Amongst the Wildflowers

the

Finding Forever Book 3

USA TODAY BESTSELLING AUTHOR

AMALI ROSE

Amongst the Wildflowers
Copyright © 2018 by Amali Rose

Editing: Ellie McLove - My Brother's Editor
Proofreading: Stacey Broadbent & Petrina Jenkins - Spell Bound
Cover Art by: Ben Ellis – Tall Story Designs
Cover Photo: Adobestock

Amongst the Wildflowers

Finding Forever Book 3

USA TODAY BESTSELLING AUTHOR
AMALI ROSE

This book is dedicated to the people who constantly strive to build others up and inspire.
You make the world a much nicer place to exist.

"In a world where you can be anything, be kind."

Synopsis

Some wallflowers are too beautiful to hide in the shadows forever.

After growing up in the shadow of her vivacious sister, Layla Jenson believed she'd never measured up, preferring to live a quiet existence, dreaming of true love while watching life pass her by.

When a member of her college football team suddenly asks her out, Layla is stunned but also hopeful. Maybe being the awkward girl who struggles socially is an endearing quality after all?

Watching Layla date his teammate is a problem for Ethan Miller. Athletic and outgoing, he's been best friends with Layla since childhood. He is the one person who *sees* her—who has always seen her. And as the stakes in the game change, Ethan is forced to face his feelings.

He's left with a single choice—admit he's in love with his best friend, or stand back and possibly lose her forever.

PROLOGUE

LAYLA

$\mathcal{M}$y legs are on fire and my lungs about to burst, but I push myself forward, distancing myself from the words. *Those words.* The hate they throw at me, making me want to curl up and disappear.

Arms pumping, I burst into the field behind my home and immediately fall in a heap amongst the beauty of the wildflowers, shoulders shaking as I purge the bitterness rioting through my body.

Seconds pass unknowingly and with each beat of my heart, the sobs wrack my body. His approach goes unseen, but I hear the rustle of flowers as he takes his place on the hard ground next to me.

Wordlessly, his pinkie finger wraps around my own and a calmness envelops me. Oblivious to time, we lie there, and I allow his steady breath to soothe me, the way his presence always does.

What could be minutes, or hours later, he stands,

unfolding his lanky frame and reaches out for me. Without hesitation I take hold, his warm, strong grasp filling me with strength.

He's got me. He's always got me.

CHAPTER ONE

LAYLA

*M*y eyes wander around the library, taking in the quiet serenity that I love so much. There is nothing in this world that beats the atmosphere of a library. The sense of peace, the smell of books and the power of knowledge held within these walls. It all combines to create a heady sense of intoxication. Casting another glance around, this time I notice a small group of girls whispering and giggling as they play around on their phones, ignoring the work scattered around in front of them.

Okay, well, it's possible it's just me that feels so strongly about them.

Sighing, my hand unconsciously finds my glasses and pushes them up the bridge of my nose before I check my phone for the eighteenth time in the last thirty minutes. The paper I'm supposed to be writing sits pointlessly on the table in front of me while I wonder where Evie could be.

Realizing my next class begins in twenty minutes

and I need to get going, I close my textbooks and begin to pack away my things, worrying my bottom lip between my teeth the entire time. It's not like Evie to stand me up.

Just as I slide the last of my things into my backpack, Evie comes barreling through the aisles toward me, huffing and puffing and garnering plenty of dirty looks on her way.

As always, I'm struck by her easy dismissal of other people's opinions. She is oblivious to the hostility she's receiving, her focus on me never wavering. I, on the other hand, can feel my face flush as her entrance throws unwanted attention my way.

"I know, I know, I know! I'm sorry, but I have a good reason, I swear!"

My eyes trail down her body, taking in her frazzled appearance. Her brown hair is pulled up in a purposefully messy bun, but it has come loose at some point and a few long tendrils are stuck to her red, sweaty face. But what immediately grabs my attention is a large red stain spread across her white t-shirt that causes me to feel slightly faint.

"Is that blood?" I can't disguise the disgust in my voice and despite my light-headedness growing worse at just the idea of a bloody wound on her abdomen, I begin planning our trip to the emergency room. What if I have to look at it? My eyes widen in horror at the thought and I plop my butt on the chair closest to me, sucking in air.

"What?" Her voice is curious as she looks down at herself and her fingers go straight to the stain, her face scrunching up in annoyance. Turning back to face me, she laughs loudly at my hunched-over-almost-hyperventilating form.

"Oh my God, relax, it's just ketchup." Evie gives me a look that is far too judgmental, in my opinion, as I process this information and feel my body return to normal.

"Lay, you do realize that you're going to be a grade school teacher, right? A teacher to tiny little germ-infested humans, who are pretty much constantly covered in some kind of bodily fluid?"

I hold my hand up to stop her as my stomach starts to drop again, but she's on a roll.

"Blood, snot, spew... oh my God, poop! You'll totally have to deal with poop at some stage! How are you going to cope?"

"You know, you're not helping my situation right now." I roll my eyes at her dramatics. "I mean, yeah, I'm not great with blood, but really? It's not like all of that will be a daily occurrence, right? I'm going to be a teacher, not a nurse."

"Whatever." She shrugs. "All I know is I used to babysit a six-year-old, and he was always covered in something disgusting. Kids are kind of gross, Lay. You need to be prepared for that shit." She laughs loudly. "Metaphorically *and* literally!"

Taking hold of my hand, she drags me along, pulling me toward the exit. "C'mon, we need to haul ass or we're going to be late to art history."

I blink against the muted sunlight as we leave the library and head toward the arts building across the quad. Fallen leaves crunch under our feet and the crispness of the air reminds me autumn is here and leaves me craving a pumpkin-spiced latte. Those things are the bomb diggity, and don't ever let anyone tell you otherwise.

I link my arm through Evie's as we stroll across campus in a much more leisurely fashion than we should. Normally, I would be racing, but our art history professor, Professor Sims, is notorious for being late to class.

"So, why were you late and why do you have that God-awful stain on your shirt?"

"Oh! I was running late because Jessie caught me after psych and wanted to borrow my notes from a class she missed. *Then* I needed to grab something from the food court, because I was starving, and this uber hottie crashed into me and smooshed his hot dog against me!" Leaning her head against mine, she waggles her eyebrows conspiratorially. "Unfortunately, I'm not speaking literally, 'cause dude was hot and I would be more than happy to acquaint myself with his hot dog, if you get my meaning."

I giggle at her lame innuendo. "Yeah, I don't think you're as subtle as you think you are."

"Aw, sugar plum, I can do graphic if that's what you prefer."

"I'm good, but thanks anyway," I answer wryly.

Evie straightens suddenly, nudging my shoulder. "Speaking of doable hot dogs, look who's over there."

I follow her gaze and spot Michael Bradshaw lounging on the grass with a group of fellow football players. My breath catches in my throat, and when I notice his head start to turn my way, I immediately avert my eyes and duck my head down.

My crush on Michael is ridiculous; I'm the first to admit this. He's the star quarterback, most popular guy on campus, and if rumors are to be believed, he is also a total manwhore. Which is exactly why he's not for me, and I shouldn't be making gooey heart eyes at him across the quad.

But he's also the first guy to make my girly senses tingle since... well, let's not go there. Suffice to say, he's the unicorn I didn't think existed, which is why I don't beat myself up too much when my eyes seek him out anytime he's within a five-mile radius. There's no harm in dreaming, right?

"When are you going to talk to him, already? You two would make such a cute couple." Evie's voice interrupts my thoughts and I barely control the snort that wants to escape in response to that little gem.

"Yeah, the hot quarterback and the chubby, plain, nerdy girl. It's a match made in heaven, I'm sure."

"Okay, I'm going to ignore the chubby, plain remark, because you're stubborn as hell, and frankly I'm tired of telling you you're sexy as fuck. But the hot quarterback and the nerd *is* a match made in heaven. Hell, I can name at least ten books off the top of my head, that proves that point."

I use every ounce of my self-control to keep my eyes from rolling. "In *books* Evie, not real life. In real life, the hot quarterback dates the hot cheerleader." I pause as I consider this. "Or he sluts around with any hot chick that will spread her legs for him. And both are perfectly valid life choices. More power to them. But nowhere do I fit in that story, and that's okay. I'm perfectly content to ogle all that pretty from afar."

"Whatever, liar. We'll talk about this later."

Fortunately, we reach the arts building and Evie lets the subject drop as we make our way into the lecture hall. The class is filling up already and the noise of raucous voices and laughter echoes around us as we take our seats at the back of the auditorium, near the door. Art History is my last class of the day, and considering it's Friday, I'm eager to make a quick exit when it's all done.

"Hey, you want to go out for a drink tonight? It's two-dollar shot night at *Hound Dog*." She eyes me beseechingly as I consider her offer. I have an English paper I really need to work on, but I really could do with a night out. Between my work at *Books & Beans* and preparing for the school year, it's been way too long since I had a bit of fun.

"Why not?"

Evie grasps my hands, her face alight with excitement. "Oh, thank God! I thought I was going to have to start bribing you with donut holes to get you out of the dorm room, and my wallet really can't handle that kind of pressure."

"Jeez, exaggerate much? I haven't been that bad." My brow furrows. "Have I?"

"Lay, you've hardly left the dorm this week. I get that it's the first week of school and you want to 'start as you mean to go on.'" My eyes narrow at her use of air quotes. "But you need to find balance. All work and no play makes you..." Her voice trails off. "Well, boring. It makes you boring, Layla." Shrugging her shoulders, she quirks an eyebrow at me.

I sigh quietly at her observation. It's possible I might have been a bit too enthusiastic this week, but it's my final year at college and I just want it to go as smoothly as possible. It seemed like a good idea to throw myself into my studies, but even I have to admit that after only five days it's already getting old. "Okay, point taken. But if you think for one second, you're getting me drunk on cheap and nasty shots, you're mistaken."

"We'll see, I guess." I do my best to ignore the mischievous tone in her voice and all its implications.

Professor Sims chooses this moment to arrive, and we go about settling in for the day's lesson while the professor's melodic voice starts going through the course syllabus.

While I am far from artistic myself, I'm a huge art lover and I have been so excited to take this course. My eyes are glued to the front of the class, keenly absorbing all the information we are being given, and my concentration is focused so completely it takes a few punches to my arm for Evie to get my attention.

"What!" I hiss as quietly as possible.

"It's him! The hottie!" She motions with her eyes to the door, and I swivel my neck to see who has her all excited.

The hairs on the back of my neck stand on end and

my heart rate doubles as I look at the guy standing there.

It couldn't be. Surely, I would have heard if he was back in town.

Unable to tear my deprived eyes away, I trail them up and down, noting and devouring everything about him. The always-mussed dark brown hair, so familiar, reminding me of the years we shared. The masculine scruff covering his jaw, so different, reminding me of the years that have passed.

His stance as he stands at the entrance to the auditorium is confident, and his bright hazel eyes are alight with amused interest as he scans the room, however his expression changes to one that could almost be described as relief as his gaze clashes with mine. My stomach drops as he immediately heads in our direction.

Glancing at Evie, I notice she is practically bouncing in her seat as she follows his path toward us. Meanwhile, I'm trying to slouch down in my own seat in an attempt to make myself invisible, desperate to avoid what I know is coming. My cheeks flame as I see a pair of black Chucks stop in front of my seat, and I slowly raise my eyes to meet his.

"Hey, Bug."

CHAPTER TWO

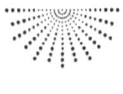

ETHAN

*T*hose eyes. Those fucking eyes kill me every time; always filled with so much uncertainty. Never with me though. Nope, there's no uncertainty in the way her eyes are narrowed and glaring at me.

I'm surprised it's taken so long to stumble on her. I've been back in town for a couple of months now, and I assumed we would have run into each other before classes started. It didn't happen though, and I was too much of a pussy to reach out and let her know I was back – scared she would look at me with the exact expression that has settled on her face right now.

"This seat taken?" I motion to the empty spot beside her. Layla's face is frozen in shock, and when I glance at the pretty brunette on her other side, I notice it's the same girl I crashed into in the food court earlier. I can't help chuckling at the way her eyes are frantically bouncing between the two of us.

Not bothering to wait for an answer, I throw myself into the seat and make myself comfortable.

"Have I missed anything important?"

The answering shake of her head is almost imperceptible, and I can see her brain working madly, trying to figure out what the fuck is going on.

The next hour crawls by painfully slowly. Layla's attention remains steadfastly focused on the front of the class, but I can feel the tension radiating off her. She's pissed. I knew she would be, but I also know she hates confrontation, and I'm banking on that helping me to win her over.

I watch the minutes tick by, not taking in any of the professor's spiel, but fuck it, it's the first class of the year and I've got more important things to worry about.

Finally, we're dismissed, and I watch from the corner of my eye as Layla quickly gathers her things and attempts to bolt. I'm quicker though, and as she turns to maneuver up from her seat, she ends up crashing right into me. My hands immediately reach out to steady her and my brow creases as I notice how much she's changed.

Not the face staring back at me, defiantly. That's exactly as I remember. Tanned and round, with a blush that always tints her cheeks. Full lips that scream of my every perverted fantasy. And then there are those eyes. Huge, warm, chocolate brown eyes that are always overflowing with emotion, unable to hide whatever she is feeling. The rest of her is completely different though, and I can't help the feeling of regret that seizes my gut. Because she was perfect. So fucking perfect, and she never even realized it.

"Can we talk? Maybe go and have a drink?"

"I don't think we have anything to talk about, Ethan." Her right eyebrow quirks, challenging me. "I mean, maybe we did three years ago, but you made it pretty clear you didn't want to talk to me, so I think I'm good. Excuse me." She attempts to push past me, but I stand firm, refusing to move.

"C'mon, Bug, don't be like that."

"Yeah, *Bug*, don't be like that. Talk to the man."

I glance at Layla's friend in gratitude. Despite the teasing tone in her voice, I'll take any support I can get. Looking past Layla, I address the friendly brunette. "Hey, I'm Ethan. Sorry again for earlier, and thanks for not holding it against me."

"Oh, Ethan." She shakes her head. "There are so many things I'd like to hold against you, but a grudge is not one of them. I'm Evie and it is delightful to meet you. Now, I have no idea what is going on here—" she motions between Layla and me, "—but sugar plum here is most certainly free for a drink. So, I'm going to leave you two to it." Turning to face Layla, who is openly glaring at her, she holds her hand up to her ear, the universal sign for phone, and mouths "call me." The only response she gets is the drop of Layla's jaw.

Straightening her back, Layla turns to face me. "One drink." Then, before I can say anything, she storms off leaving me behind. Let's hope that's not a fucking omen.

Twenty minutes later we're in some tiny little juice bar, cramped in amongst a dozen other tables. Every time I move, I elbow the girl sitting behind me, and from the look in her eye, I'm about to get a right hook to my face if I can't keep still.

Layla is sitting across from me, her straw rolling between her fingers as she uses it to make waves in her OJ. She hasn't spoken a word to me, and it's clear she's not going to make this easy. I don't really deserve easy, though, so I can deal with that.

My stomach is churning and I'm trying to decide how to start when I notice her eyes flick to the clock above the counter. I guess I'm all out of time.

"I'm sorry, Bug. I was an asshole."

Her gaze remains locked on her drink, but I hear the tiny, "Yep," she exhales out.

Taking a deep breath, I do the only thing I can and push on. "It was a dick thing to do and I don't have any excuse. I wish I did."

Her hand stills and I see her shoulders slump slightly at my words. The silence stretches, and I can feel my anxiety build while I wait for her response. I've completely turned my life upside down in the last few months, transferring colleges and leaving a life I loved behind. And I did it for one reason, and one reason only. Layla. Because I've realized that no matter how great my life is, if it doesn't include her in some capacity, it feels like I'm only living half a life.

"What did I do wrong?" Her voice is barely a whisper, but I hear her, and I swear to God, those five

14

words are like a punch to my chest, the pain radiating through my entire body.

"*Shit.* You didn't do anything, Bug." I lean forward on the table, trying to make eye contact so I can make her see my truth. The only truth I'm prepared to give her right now. "I got caught up in the freedom of not having to answer to anyone, of being around people who didn't know me and had no expectations of me. I got so busy creating a new life that I forgot about my old one, and that makes me an asshole, I know. I'm sorry."

There's a beat of silence before she raises her head to look at me. A single beat where I still have hope that she'll flash me a smile and forgive me for being a douchebag. A lonely beat before she opens that lush mouth of hers, and my hope is crushed.

"You were my best friend, Ethan. You were my person. The one who, no matter what else was going on in my life, made me feel like it was going to be okay. Like *I* was going to be okay. Then, completely out of the blue, you decide you need to go to college out of state." She pauses and takes a deep, steadying breath before continuing. "I tried *so* hard to be supportive. I understood why you wanted to leave, and no matter how hard it was going to be for me to be without you, I wanted you to have that chance." She abruptly pushes her juice away as she straightens in her seat, a look of pain locking on her face. "But when you began to shut me out and make me feel like I was just one more obligation you were stuck dealing with, you hurt me in a way I never thought you could. I never expected anything from you except the truth, and you couldn't even give me that."

I can't take my eyes off her, and when her voice wavers, it takes all my self-control not to blurt out exactly why I had done what I had.

When she continues, her tone is quietly determined. "You destroyed me, Ethan, and I don't think I can forgive you for that. I'm sorry."

With that, she quickly gathers her things and I'm left alone watching her walk away. And I let her go because I have no idea how to justify my actions without confessing my biggest secret. That I had to leave, because loving her was destroying me.

CHAPTER THREE

LAYLA

Two days later, I'm lying on my bed in a silent dorm room, staring at the ceiling. Normally, I would love this moment of calm; a small reprieve from the noise that follows Evie around. Tonight, though, it's exacerbating the chaos in my head. The chaos that hasn't stopped since I walked away from Ethan on Friday.

My teeth latch on to my plump lower lip and begin gnawing away while I try to get my head straight. I've learned over time that there will always be people in life who will hurt you. Those people who you care about and all they do is take from you. Those people who you open up to and put your trust in, only for them to abuse it. The people you wish you meant something to, but you're only ever a diversion to be enjoyed until they get bored and move on. I've known plenty of these people, but I never, for one second, believed he would be one of them.

Until the day he was.

I was so unprepared to see him. *So* unprepared for all the feelings that overwhelmed me. I thought I had made peace with his vanishing act years ago but seeing him stand in front of me brought all the pain rushing back. It made me realize exactly how much I have missed him. I'm still not sure how I found the strength to walk away.

Or how I'll find the strength to *stay* away.

The peace and quiet is shattered as Evie bursts through the door, almost dropping a pile of textbooks on her way.

"Oh, Jesus, if I ever see another textbook as long as I live, it'll be too soon." She dumps her books on the small desk before flopping down on the bed and pointing a finger angrily at me. "You!"

"Me?"

"Yes, you! Don't think I don't realize you've been avoiding me, young lady. Now, spill. How do you know my uber hottie?"

I can't help the small giggle that escapes. "Seriously, please never refer to him as that to his face. His ego was always big enough."

"Okay, I want *all* the details. *Then* I want you to beg for my forgiveness for never telling me you had an ex that looks like *that*."

"Oh God, he's not my ex! We were only ever friends." Her eyes narrow suspiciously.

"How in the hell do you stay just friends with a guy who looks like that? I'm pretty sure it's not physically possible. Like, 'oops! Sorry, I fell, and my mouth accidentally landed on your dick. My bad!'"

I snort out a laugh. "That's a pretty solid plan you have there, sweet cheeks." The smile slides from my face as quickly as it came, and my eyes burn with the unwanted sensation of the tears I've been holding back for two days.

"Lay?" Before I can reply, Evie is crawling on my bed with me, pushing me over and squishing me into the wall, before she takes hold of my hand. "You liked him?"

I want to scoff at her use of the word *like*. Because it is so much more complex than that. Like is too easy for what we have. I've loved him since I was four years old. I've been *in* love with him since I was twelve. And I have been broken by him since I was eighteen.

Taking a deep breath, I try to calm my mind enough to explain it to her.

"When I was four, I was lying in the field behind my house, crying. Like, full-on sobbing, because a group of girls wouldn't let me play with them. They said I was too ugly to be a princess." Evie's grip on my hand tightens. "So, I'm lying there, feeling like my heart is breaking, trying to figure out how I can possibly make myself pretty enough, when suddenly this beautiful blue flower is shoved in my face." My lips tilt in a small smile as the memory comes flooding back. "I turned around and there he was, asking if I would be his friend." I roll over onto my side and face her, smiling at the memory. "He had just moved in next door, and from that day on he was just always there. He became my best friend, my protector. And one day I realized he had become my everything."

Evie's brow creases in confusion. "Okay, so I'm confused. How did you get from there to here?"

My answering sigh is full of frustration. "I have no freaking idea. At the end of our senior year, he just started pulling away. Like, he was there, but he wasn't, if you know what I mean. He stopped talking to me about anything that wasn't superficial crap and then one day he told me that he had decided to go to college in Washington." I flinch slightly at the memory. "I didn't even know he was considering moving out of state."

"You never asked him why he was acting differently or called him out on it?" Evie's nose crinkles in confusion.

"I think I was scared to. Like I've said before, school wasn't easy for me. I got teased a lot—"

"Bullied. The word is bullied, Lay. You went to school with a bunch of assholes."

I smile sadly at her blunt words. "Yeah, I really did." Shaking my head, I continue. "Anyway, I guess I was worried that if I confronted him about it, I would lose him completely. Even though I hated that he was slowly slipping away, at least I still had some of him. Does that make sense?" Evie nods silently.

"I figured he would tell me when he was ready. He would explain what had changed, but he never did. Then he was gone, and I was still clueless. I tried to stay in touch, but it was pretty obvious he wasn't interested. So, I did what I thought he wanted, and left him alone." The memories of waiting for messages that never came, calls that went unanswered and unreturned assault me, and the pain is just as intense now as it was then. "I always figured he would get in touch eventually, but one month turned into six, which turned into a year and I realized I had to get over it and move on, so I did my best to make that happen."

"How did I not know all of this? I'm your room-mate. We're best friends! You could have talked to me, you know."

I do my best to ignore the note of hurt in Evie's voice. "It was too hard to talk about. You not knowing kind of gave me a bit of respite from being miserable. There was so much change happening in my life. But you." I wrap my arms around her in an awkward attempt at a hug. "Were my happy place, Evie Mitchell."

"Ugh, okay, you're forgiven." She jumps off the bed with a grace that I envy, all long limbs and flowing hair. I swear if I didn't love her so much I'd hate her.

"So, what are you going to do about Ethan? Is he forgiven too?" she asks as she pulls a water from our mini-fridge under the desk.

I try to figure out how to answer her honestly, while still holding onto a shred of dignity. Because I will forgive him. I already know I will. Despite what I said and despite what he did, he is so intrinsically entwined with my heart I have no idea how to live without him. I've proven that I can exist, but living? I never quite mastered that.

"I'm not sure what I'm going to do. I have no idea how to be around him and not be *us*, but I also have no idea how to pretend that I'm not still angry at him."

"So, don't pretend." Her shoulders lift in a careless

shrug. "Tell him you're pissed but don't shut the door on him either. Maybe you can't go back to being BFFs, but you can start trying to build something new. It might not be the same, but if he meant as much to you as you say, then isn't *something* better than nothing?"

I watch her thoughtfully as she chugs down her water before I reply. "You know, you're not just a pretty face."

"Right? I'm a hot piece of ass too, don't ever forget that." When she winks at me across the room, I don't even try to hide my groan.

The gravel crunches under my feet and Selena Gomez blasts in my ears as I make my way along the jogging path across the campus. Unable to shut my brain off last night, I had trouble falling asleep and ended up snoozing right through my alarm, which explains why I'm so late on my daily run *and* why I'm so grumpy. Not a morning person at the best of times, the lack of sleep only heightens my annoyance with all the people swanning around, getting in my way as I try to navigate my usual route. When a guy with his eyes glued to his cell phone carelessly cuts me off, I huff in exasperation and decide to cut my losses and jog back to the dorm. Just as I'm about to make a left and head back, I spot the campus coffee shop up ahead and decide to stop and grab a water.

Standing in front of the cooler, I am reaching for a bottle when a head pops into my periphery, startling the crud out of me, almost causing me to drop my water.

"Oh, jeez!" Turning and removing my headphones, I realize it's Ethan. My stomach drops and my heart races simultaneously. He's looking behind me quizzically, as though searching for something, and I have to bite my lip to hide the smile that wants to break free. Instead, I do my best to appear unaffected while pushing my sweaty hair back self-consciously.

"What are you looking for?"

"I seem to remember you showing me a meme years ago that said something along the lines of if I see you running, then I should run too, because something must be chasing you. So, what is it, Bug? You need me to save you from a rogue bear or something? 'Cause I'll do it." I laugh at the memory of fifteen-year-old Ethan trying to persuade me to go running with him, and my steadfast refusal.

"You were on your meme game that day." He wears a soft smile that makes me remember everything I probably shouldn't right now.

"Well, it was hard to keep up with Millhouse the meme king. I did what I could."

"Christ, I haven't been called that in so long." He smirks at the memory of the nickname I gave him when we were ten years old and he went through a brief obsession with the show *The Simpsons*. "I still say I'm a Bart."

"Pfft, whatever, *Millhouse*." A small nudge to my shoulder as someone squeezes past us reminds me where we are, and I start to move off in the direction of the register. Ethan gently takes hold of my arm to stop me.

"When's your first class? Do you have time for a coffee?"

He's looking at me so hopefully, and I can't deny that I want to stay talking to him. Remembering Evie's words about finding a new normal, I decide to dive in head-first. "Uh, sure, I have a little time."

Five minutes later, I'm sitting opposite the guy who was my best friend for fourteen years. The guy I shared every detail of my life with. And it. Is. So. Freaking. Awkward.

Ethan's eyes look everywhere but at me and even though the coffee shop is bustling for seven in the morning, our silence is deafening, and I'm reconsidering my decision to stay.

"So, peppermint tea, huh?" he abruptly blurts out. Yep, still reconsidering.

"Yeah, I gave up coffee a few years ago."

"What? You were a caffeine fiend. I was honestly terrified of you before you had your first cup of the day."

"Oh my God, I wasn't that bad, you big baby." I roll my eyes. "I decided to make some changes a few years ago. Improve myself, I guess. Ditching the caffeine was a part of it."

"That's where the running and—" he uses his index finger to motion toward me, "—*that* comes in?"

"That?"

"The new body." The ever-present blush stains my cheeks even darker at his words. Calm yourself, Jensen, it's just an observation. He will never see you that way, so don't even go there.

"Well, the old body wasn't really working for me, so I figured it was about time I made improvements."

Ethan's playing with an empty sugar packet, his fingers tearing shreds off it and his voice is quiet when he responds.

"There was never anything wrong with you, Layla."

My answering snort is unconscious. "You were the only one who ever thought so. And then you were gone." I shrug, but my heart clenches when I notice him deflate slightly at my careless comment, so I hurry to undo the hurt. "*I* didn't like myself very much, so I tried to change what needed to change, so I would. It's not really a big deal." He closes his eyes briefly, but when he looks up, he is distracted by something over my shoulder.

"Fuck," he says with a grimace.

"What?" I throw a glance over my shoulder and spot Michael Bradshaw walking toward us, a sly smile gracing his full mouth.

Oh. Crud.

CHAPTER FOUR

ETHAN

*M*y temper flares as that fuckwit Bradshaw makes his way toward us. I swear to God, I'm about ready to punch that smug smile off his face if he takes one more step in our direction.

Clearly, he's not a smart guy because despite the grimace I know I'm wearing, his course never falters.

"Miller, man, I'm glad I ran into you." My shoulder stings under his 'friendly' back slap. Yep, this asshole is going down.

"What do you want, Bradshaw?" I note the look of disapproval on Layla's face at my tone, but if she knew this guy, she would understand.

I feel my hands clench into fists when Michael turns his attention to Layla.

"Hey, Layla, right?" Her face reddens under his gaze and when she nods, ducking her head down shyly, a red haze engulfs me.

"I'm busy, just tell me what you want."

I don't miss the antagonistic look that flits over his face when he realizes what's bugging me.

"Relax, dude. I just wanted to let you know that the team is going to *Hound Dog* tonight for a couple of drinks. Let's call it team building." He turns his attention to Bug. "You should come; the other girlfriends are."

Her eyes flick to mine. Jesus, does she have to look so fucking horrified at the thought?

"Oh, we're not –we're just friends."

"Really?" His look turns predatory, his chances of living through this conversation dwindling. "You should definitely come, then."

"Thanks for letting me know," I interrupt his eye-fucking and unapologetically wait for him to leave. When he doesn't move, I decide to bypass subtlety completely. "You can leave now."

Michael chuckles before throwing his hands up in defeat. "Alright, I can take a hint. I wouldn't want to share her either." My eyes narrow as I watch Layla's face flush an even deeper shade of red at his comment. Asshole.

"See you both tonight." I watch his retreating back silently. This is going to be harder than I thought if I have to watch fuckers like that hit on her all the time. I may have to start saving for bail money.

Picking up my coffee, I turn back to Layla and see that she is also watching Bradshaw leave. Although, I'd bet my last dollar that the expression on my face is very different to the one hers is wearing right now.

"So, *Hound Dog* tonight?" I hate the hopeful note I

hear in my voice. Even more, I hate that I'm the one responsible for this distance between us.

Layla appears to be considering the idea, so I push on. "You can bring Evie and we can catch up." Watching her closely, I can see that I've almost got her. "C'mon, Bug, just a few drinks. I promise you'll be home, curled up in bed with your Kindle before you know it."

When she rolls her eyes at me, I have to restrain myself from fist-pumping.

"Fine. But only because Evie would slaughter me painfully if she found out I turned down an invite from Michael Bradshaw."

Her words are like a punch to the gut and I have to work to seem unaffected. The awkwardness is cut off when her phone begins jumping around the table, some pop song playing loudly, offending my ears. Looking down, I see a picture of Layla's sister, Cassidy, light up the screen and I can't control the huge smile I now sport. That girl is batshit crazy.

"Give me one second, I'll be right back." Snatching up her phone, she's answering before she's even reached the door.

I rub my hands roughly up and down my face, my stubble scratching my coarse hands as I replay the encounter with Bradshaw in my mind. My plan was only to get from Layla what she was happy to give me. Do I want my best friend back? Abso-fucking-lutely. Will I settle for less? Bet your ass I will. But if I have to watch her date dickholes like Michael, I'm not sure this is going to end well. It was my jealousy that started this whole mess, and I really need to figure out how to rein it in, if I have any hope of finding a way to be just friends with the girl I've loved since I was four years old.

"I have no idea how we're sisters." She appears out of nowhere, falling onto her chair and startling me out of my thoughts.

A slow smile spreads across my face as I remember all the crazy shit Cassidy has pulled over the years. "How's CJ doing?"

"She's good." Her eyes roll. "She's started a new job and she hates her boss. She was calling to get ideas for practical jokes, so it's probably safe to say she won't be working there much longer." Picking up her cup, she drinks down the remains. "I have to get going if I'm going to make my first class." She stands, attaching her armband and putting her earphones in before pausing. "We'll meet you at *Hound Dog* at eight?"

I lock down my smirk. "Sounds good."

"Okay, see ya then." With that, she turns, and my eyes follow as she sways that curvy ass of hers out the door.

Shit. I'm in so much fucking trouble.

Four years earlier...

"Miller!" A hand slams my locker shut and I jerk back just in time, the door barely missing my head. I glare over my

shoulder at Levi Calder, my best friend and sometimes-douchebag.

"What the hell, dude?" My right shoulder sags slightly under the weight of my backpack, Layla's chemistry textbooks weighing it down. Those fuckers are heavy. I start walking toward the exit, pushing through the wave of people all fighting to escape these halls and kick off their weekend, away from classrooms, teachers and the endless rules we're forced to live by throughout the week.

Levi follows close behind, yammering on about some party tonight at Nichola Brennan's house.

He finally pauses and takes a damn breath. "So, you gonna come?"

I exhale harshly and consider my options. Nichola's parents are what you call permissive parents. Which basically means this party will be high on fun and low on parental figures. It also means I'll never be able to convince Layla to go with me.

"I'll stop by for a while."

"Good. You need to talk to Jasmine, man. Now that she's broken up with Sully, word is she wants you to take her to the prom. And I heard that pussy can choke a dick better than any other out there, so you're gonna want to get on that."

"Yeah, not gonna happen."

"Why the hell not?" His voice is a combination of incredulous and antagonistic, and I already know what's coming.

"I'm taking Layla to prom."

Levi's snort of disgust is immediate. "Jesus Christ, when are you going to stop worrying about that heifer?"

Before I even realize what I'm doing, I have his collar

bunched in my fists and have him thrown up against the wall, using every bit of my strength.

"The fuck did you just say, asshole?"

Levi's face is red and straining, but once he regains composure, he's pushing me back, trying to get free. "Get off me, you dick."

I notice the students around us have stopped and are watching our confrontation intently, some with phones pointed in our direction, which means a teacher won't be far behind, so I loosen my grip.

"I ever hear you talk about her like that again and I will fucking end you, Calder, you got it?" I shove him away and move quickly toward the parking lot. The douche can kiss my ass.

Exiting the building, I tilt my head slightly to meet the sun, hoping it will calm the rage in my head. It doesn't, and that motherfucker is lucky he's still alive.

Glancing up, I spot Bug leaning against my car, waiting, her face buried in her Kindle. The grin that spreads across my face is instinctive. The tension drains from my body and I pick up speed as I cross the parking lot to get to her.

Leaning down, I plant a kiss on her neck causing her to jump.

"Reading a dirty book on school grounds, Bug? You're getting pretty blatant with your perversions, aren't you?"

Her nose scrunches up in indignation. "Bite me, Millhouse."

I tsk, slowly shaking my head. "Biting, Layla? You really are becoming corrupted."

She laughs, pushes her glasses up the bridge of her nose, and flips me the bird before climbing into the car. As I settle behind the steering wheel, Levi passes by in front of us and he glares at me through the windshield. Out of the corner of my eye, I see Layla's head turn toward me, but I keep my attention focused on starting the ignition and getting us out of here.

It's only a matter of minutes before Layla begins wiggling around in her seat and I can feel her impatience radiating off her in waves.

"Do you need to pee?" I toss a quick glance her way. "Do I need to pull over?"

Her eyes narrow in confusion. "What? Why would I need to pee? And why would you think I would ever pee on the side of the road? What have I ever done to indicate I'm a pee-by-the-side-of-the-road kind of girl?"

"Well, the way you're wiggling around over there, I figured it had to be the only explanation."

"Don't be a smartass, Ethan, it doesn't become you."

"I think you'll find any kind of ass becomes me. It's one of my best features, all the girls think so."

She remains silent, but I can imagine her rolling her eyes in exasperation. Wanting to get the full impact, I turn toward her. Instead of seeing the humorous exasperation I expected, she is staring out the window, her jaw clenched, looking contemplative.

"Bug?"

She turns to face me with a small smile. "So, speaking of butts, what's up Levi's? He looked pretty angry."

"Nothing." My hands tighten on the wheel.

"Riiiiight. Because that looked like nothing." This time I get my eye roll and she pauses briefly before continuing. "Anyway, I have some news."

"Yeah? Please tell me you finally found your Taylor Swift CD? Because that has just been keeping me up at night." The punch to my arm is swift (no pun intended) and well deserved. Especially considering said CD is lying on the bottom of my closet, hidden under a pile of trash. Where it belongs.

"Shut up! You just wish you had my exceptional taste in music!"

"Yeah, that's definitely it." I snort as I pull into my driveway. I turn off the engine and turn to face her. "Okay, what's your news L-swizzle?"

Her face flushes suddenly and her grin is replaced by a pensive look.

"Luke Cameron asked me to the prom."

My ears start to ring, and I wonder if it's possible that I misheard her.

"What?" I bark out. My tone is harsher than I intended, and she flinches slightly. Confrontation isn't Layla's thing and she does whatever she can to avoid it. Unfortunately for her, she can't avoid this.

"I thought we were going to prom together, Lay. What the fuck?"

Her hand finds my arm and she squeezes it in an attempt to calm me.

"I know we were. And I love you for wanting to take me, but he asked, so I said yes." She shrugs, as if it's no big deal, while my mind is racing a mile a minute trying to place this Cameron fucker and decide how I'm going to kill him.

"This is perfect, Ethan. You can go with one of the hotties that are always trying to get in your pants, and I'll go with Luke. You never know." She waggles her eyebrows at me. "I

might get to practice some of the dirty stuff I read about."
Before I can think of a response, let alone verbalize one, she
is out of the car and heading toward my house, completely
oblivious to the chaos rioting within me.

🐾

"Babe, did you make sure you got the double-stuffed Oreos this time?"

I'm barely in the door when my roommate, Seth's voice hollers at me.

Looking up, I see him, ass glued to the sofa, eyes locked on the television screen and controller in hand.

"We have regular Oreos in the pantry. You'll eat them, and you'll enjoy them. *Babe.*"

A lazy smirk crosses his face as he glances at me. "Mia never remembers double-stuffed. I mean who the hell wants regular Oreos? I've sent her twenty-three messages reminding her and she hasn't bothered replying to any. Bet your ass she walks in here with the regular ones." His face creases in disgust at the thought. "But what's got your panties in such a bunch, princess?"

My legs make quick work of the space between the door and the sofa and I flop down next to him, throwing my backpack on the ground angrily. Rolling my shoulders, I attempt to release the tension that's pervaded my body since my encounter with Michael Bradshaw this morning.

"Bradshaw's an asshole, right? I'm not the only one who thinks so?"

"Fuck no, that guy's the biggest douche I've ever had

the bad luck to meet. If he wasn't the captain of the football team, he'd be the most hated guy on campus." Keeping his eyes on the screen in front of him, he throws me a controller and sets up a game. "Why, what'd he do?"

I groan loudly, remembering the way his eyes ate Layla up. "I was talking to Lay this morning, and he practically fucked her right in front of me."

Seth side-eyes me while still managing to kill me onscreen. That's motherfucking skill, right there.

"Really?" I choose to ignore the skeptical tone to his voice. "Because that seems unlikely."

"Well, he may as well have." I pout like a fucking child. "He invited her to *Hound Dog* tonight."

Seth's head snaps around, his eyes wide as they meet mine. "Does this mean I'm finally going to meet the girl that has you all pussy whipped?"

"Seriously, *you're* calling *me* pussy whipped? Didn't I walk in on Mia plucking your eyebrows last week?"

He grins back at me. "What can I say? My girl likes me to look my best." He shrugs as I snort out a laugh. It's impossible to embarrass this guy.

"Whatever. She'll be there. Because *Michael* invited her." My grimace is involuntary. My clenched fists, not so much.

"Who the fuck cares *why* she's coming. She's coming, which means you get to spend time with her, so quit bitching. Pull your big-girl panties on and tell her you're not interested in being her friend and offer her a ride to pound town." He shakes his head in exasperation, eyeing me like a punk.

"Oh my God, please do not say the words *pound town* to her."

Our heads whip around to find Mia standing by the door with a look of horror on her face. She turns her attention to Seth, and before I can say 'where the hell did you come from', she's throwing a package at her boyfriend's head.

"Double-stuffed Oreos, asshole," she snaps and makes her way to the kitchen.

Seth throws his hands up in the air. "Parker for the win.

CHAPTER FIVE

LAYLA

The vibration of the music hits me as soon as we walk through the door. You wouldn't think the place would be so busy on a Monday night, but you would be wrong.

"Do you see him?" Evie's mouth is just inches from my ear, but I still have to strain to hear her.

"Ethan?" I search the crowd, my eyes scanning the heads looking for his familiar mess of brown hair. "No, do you?"

A sharp elbow to my side draws my attention back to her.

"Not Ethan, Michael!"

"Michael? Are you talking about Michael Bradshaw?" Natasha, the third part of our trio interrupts, her face lit up with interest.

"Uh huh, he invited Layla." Evie's smirk holds a smidge of vindication.

"What? You didn't tell me that!" Her voice is laced

with indignation. "You told me some old school friend invited you."

"He did, I mean Michael invited him and then said I could come, but only because I was there." I don't know why I try to play down what happened this morning. It's not like Michael was subtle; even I couldn't write off his flirting as harmless. All I know is that as much as I love Tash, she has a way of making me feel small. It's not her fault, it's not malicious, it's just who she is. But I wanted to enjoy this feeling for a little while longer and not have her ruin it.

"Oh, yeah, that's totally a pity invite, babe." Yeah, exactly like that.

My stomach drops as I am suddenly grabbed from behind, two strong arms encircling my waist and lifting my feet off the ground. A warm mouth finds the spot that every woman loves, the curve where neck meets shoulder and a kiss sets every synapse on fire.

I should be alarmed, but I know this touch. It warms my entire body, inciting a reckless desire that is so familiar it mildly terrifies me.

"You made it."

Turning, I pull back slightly so I can look Ethan in the face. His bright hazel eyes are smiling, and I can't help the affection that sweeps through me.

"I told you I would. You remember Evie." I take hold of Natasha's hand and pull her closer. "And this is Tash, she lives in the dorms with us."

My stomach clenches as I watch Tash's slow perusal of Ethan's body and the way her tongue peeks out, swiping along her bottom lip in a move that almost has me ready to lay a kiss on her.

Ethan's eyes barely stray from my own as he throws out a casual hello.

"C'mon, we have a table over here." Pulling on my hand, he drags me across the room and I quickly look over my shoulder to make sure Evie and Tash are following. When I see Evie, I note the small smile on her face and I'm trying to figure out what it means when I suddenly crash into Ethan. Standing in front of a booth already occupied by a gorgeous couple, his body is all hard muscle against my own, and my hand brushes along his hip as I attempt to steady myself. A blush burns my cheeks when I feel his jeans hanging low, and my fingers tingle as they rest on that V muscle of his that has always made my core clench in the most delicious way.

I snatch my hand back and immediately search his face, hoping he didn't notice my physical reaction. Thankfully, his expression is one of blissful ignorance and while that should bring me relief, I find myself tiptoeing on the edge of annoyance, frustrated that even now he doesn't see me the way he sees every other girl. No matter how much I wish it wasn't true, I'll always be just Bug.

"Ladies, this is Seth, my roommate, and his girl-friend, Mia. Guys, this is Layla, Evie, and Tash." We exchange greetings and get ourselves situated before Ethan and Seth bring over a round of drinks. We launch into easy conversation and I'm feeling remark-ably relaxed, which is unusual for me when I meet new people. Seth and Mia are great, but I do find the attention they're lavishing on me slightly disconcerting. I'm much more content in the background while Evie and Tash shine, which is usually how our nights out go.

Also unsettling me is the way Tash has sidled up to Ethan and is attempting to engage him in conversation. She has her body pressed right up against him, her breasts rubbing against his arm and her mouth unnecessarily close to the shell of his ear as she talks to him.

He, on the other hand, is dividing his attention between our conversation and Tash's murmurings. I'm intrigued at how well I can still read him; his frustration with her attempt at seduction is clear to me. The slight furrow of his brow and the straight line of his back screams his discomfort, but to anyone else, he simply looks focused on the people around him.

"Layla, you have to tell me what Ethan was like when he was a kid. He was a loser, right? The most unpopular boy in school?" Seth's teasing voice causes me to laugh out loud at the irony of his question.

"Uh, no. Ethan was Mr. Popularity. I was the loser riding the coattails in that friendship."

Ethan's eyes cloud over at my words and my grin slips in confusion. This cannot possibly be news to him.

"Come and help me get the next round." He motions toward the bar with a slight incline of his head.

"Coke for me, please, and a water for him," Mia points to Seth. "I plan on getting laid tonight, so no whiskey dick, thank you very much."

"Fuck, yeah." Seth raises his hand to high five her.

"No." Mia's eyes narrow as she shuts him down.

"Right." He lowers his hand. "Don't want to risk spraining this bad boy. I get it." Mia's expression has me giggling as we climb out of the booth.

Making our way across the bar, Ethan positions himself protectively in front of me, blocking the hectic movement of bodies, and taking my hand.

Warmth spreads through me, his touch reminding me of home and filling me with that same feeling of comfort and familiarity. I have to work hard not to lose myself in it.

Ordering our drinks takes longer than I expected, and we are left standing side by side while we wait. I'm grateful things aren't as awkward as they were this morning, allowing me to just enjoy the feel of him without overthinking.

"You know, I never thought that." His voice is low, slightly harsh and he is looking intently at his hands clasped tightly to the bar, rather than at me.

"What?"

"I never thought you were a loser." His eyes meet mine and I'm surprised by the vulnerability I can see. "I only ever thought you were exceptional."

I try to take a moment to process what he said, but he rushes on before I can put any real thought into it.

"Leaving you like that was a huge mistake, *such* a dick thing to do and I'll probably always regret that. But I need you to know it had nothing to do with you, and I'm sorry. So sorry."

A sigh escapes me, and I feel the harsh bite of the

bar in my back as I consider how to respond. Ultimately there's no question. I need to be honest.

"It sucked. I won't tell you it didn't, but it's not like I fought that hard for our friendship. I was too busy being angry to actually do anything that could have fixed the situation."

We are interrupted by the arrival of our drinks and Ethan goes straight for his beer, taking a long pull. I can see his mind working a mile a minute over my admission, and the need to know what is going on in there is overwhelming.

He turns to me slowly, and his eyes search mine. I desperately wish I knew what he was looking for, because in this moment, I would do anything to give it to him.

"How about we start over? Our friendship meant everything to me, Bug." He offers me a small shake of his head. "But we're different people now; older. We've both changed a lot over the past four years. Maybe it's time our relationship did too."

I feel my brow furrow in confusion as I process what he's saying. Until realization dawns and my face heats with embarrassment. Of course. Having a female best friend would get in the way of the female kitty parade.

"Definitely, yep, of course." My words sound forced and while I am making every effort to sound nonchalant, I only succeed in sounding flustered.

Ethan always had a long line of girls wanting to date him, but in high school, he was exceedingly picky. I guess he doesn't have that problem anymore and I give myself a mental shake at my stupidity. I'm not sure how ready I am to see him screwing around with girls that I could never compete with; my chest pinches with pain at the simple thought.

"Hey, what's wrong?"

"What? Nothing, why?"

His hand closes around my own and I see the small crescent indentations from my thumbnail on my fingertips. An unfortunate habit when I feel anxious.

"Did I say something wron—" His words are cut off and our attention is diverted to the entrance where a small group of the football team has just arrived, noise and fanfare greeting them.

I spot Michael leading the pack, his eyes bouncing around the bar, searching for something. Or someone, as it turns out. Because when his gaze lands on me, a smile of satisfaction crosses his face and he lifts his hand in a wave.

I feel Ethan stiffen beside me and I wonder again, what he has against Michael. Their run-in this morning made it blatantly obvious he didn't care for him.

Before I can dwell on it, Michael is heading our way, a heated look in his eyes. A week ago, I would have paid good money to see Michael Bradshaw look at me like that. Now, the closer he gets, determination pulsing in every step, all I can think is how very wrong it feels.

CHAPTER SIX

ETHAN

*T*he next three hours drag by interminably as I'm forced to watch Bradshaw all over Layla. She looks uncomfortable with all his attention, as well as his horde of loser friends, causing my body to tense relentlessly with frustration.

It's moments like this that I hate her need to people-please. Hate that instead of pushing the asshole away, she forces a smile and tolerates his less-than-subtle touches. Hides the small flinch when his lips graze against her ear and he whispers something that sets her face aflame.

And most of all, I detest the way she ducks her head to disguise her embarrassment when the dickwad draws attention to the beautiful blush of her cheeks and makes a joke at her expense.

I'm grateful that Evie hasn't left her side, that she has been a constant touchstone for Layla. I've watched, completely intrigued, as they communicated effort-lessly, wordlessly. A gentle squeeze of a hand and Evie would pipe up with a ridiculous story or ask a question that would feed Michael's ego and put his attention right back where he preferred it. On himself.

A seemingly casual glance, where a furrowed brow that went unnoticed by the rest of the table, had Evie dragging Layla away for a brief respite.

I watch all of this, my gut churning with a reckless combination of gratitude and regret, and I, unfairly, wonder how long it took her to replace me. How easily she found a new safe place, and if she ever mourned my loss the way I did her.

By the time Layla's attempt to sneak away with a quiet goodbye is thwarted by Bradshaw's dramatic pleas for her to stay, my already frayed temper, heatre by more alcohol than was possibly a good idea, snaps.

"Jesus Christ, just let her go! Can't you see she's tired of your annoying ass and is trying to escape!" Hours of pent-up frustration lace my words with a venom I hadn't intended.

While the crowd around us continues to throb with the noises you expect to hear in a bar, our table is completely silent as my outburst settles.

My eyes remain fixated on my beer while I feel the weight of silent stares suffocating me from every angle.

Finally, I look up, daring anyone to contradict me, before I seek out Layla. She is in a half-standing half-crouching limbo and she looks absolutely horrified.

Regret immediately slams into me, tightening my chest painfully as I drag my gaze away, returning it to the beer in front of me.

"Well, on that cheery note, we'll be off." Evie

successfully manages to diffuse the tension and draws a round of low chuckles from the group followed by a chorus of goodbyes.

A gentle hand on my arm gains my attention and I look up to see Layla looking at me with an expression I don't recognize. This only pisses me off further. I used to know all her expressions. Every. Single. Fucking. One.

"Bye, Ethan." Her voice is soft, and I want to hear it again. I want to hear her say my name again. But I'm too wound up, so I sullenly refuse to answer.

The hand on my arm tightens, nails digging in, and I flinch slightly, my eyes snapping to hers. This expression I know, and despite the inappropriateness, I feel a grin slide across my face.

"Don't be a jerk, Ethan. Say goodbye." She is glaring at me, frustration and annoyance playing on her beautiful face, and I wish I could stare at her for hours. Days. Weeks.

"Bye, Bug." She nods once, satisfied. Then, with no further preamble, she walks away.

Dragging my attention away from the graceful sway of Layla's ass, I turn to find Michael smirking at me from across the table and notice that there is a prevailing sense of tension lingering over the group.

Refusing to give him what he wants, I push away from the table, determined to head to the bar for another drink.

Seth grabs my arm, stopping me in my tracks. "You sure that's a good idea?"

"Since when did you become Mister Fucking Responsible, Parker?" I bark.

He raises his hands in surrender, but I don't miss the look of worry he exchanges with Mia. I choose to ignore it, instead pushing my way through the crowd to get to the bar and find a refuge.

Making myself comfortable, I settle in along the bar, determined to stay here until Mia decides it's time for us to leave. Which, considering her expression a few minutes ago, shouldn't be long.

I feel a hand clamp down on my shoulder and I turn expecting to see Seth. Instead, I come face to face with fucking Bradshaw.

Ignoring him, I turn away to watch the crowd around us, and my eyes are immediately drawn to a couple holed up in a dark corner. Their bodies are pressed up against each other, their attention locked on each other, oblivious to the madness of the crowd around them. There's an intensity there, a palpable ferocity, and I realize how acutely I wish that was Layla and me.

The guy reaches up and tucks a strand of hair behind the girl's ear before slowly tracing a finger along her bottom lip, and it's that intimate gesture that has me shaking my head and realizing what a fucking creeper I'm being.

Turning back, I can't help the sigh of frustration that escapes when I see the asswipe still standing there, a look of fierce antagonism clouding his features.

"So, that Layla's a nice piece of ass. I should probably buy you a drink to thank you for bringing her around, Miller. I think the team is going to enjoy making her acquaintance." I squeeze my eyes tight in an effort to control myself.

"You will stay the fuck away from her." I force the words out through gritted teeth, my clenched fists making it perfectly clear how serious I am.

Taking a pull on his beer, he waves me off with his other hand.

"I know what you're thinking. I know."

For a second I think he's going to have the nerve to try and convince me that his intentions are honorable.

I was wrong.

"She's fatter than the girls I normally fuck. And you're right. She is. But that mouth, dude. That fucking mouth. I'll put up with a little extra junk in the trunk to see that mouth wrapped around my cock, sucking down all my cum. I'll even—"

My fist cuts him off as it slams into his jaw and I hear the satisfying crunch of bone against bone before he slumps to the ground, caught off guard.

I'm about to drag him back up so I can throw a second punch when I'm pulled backward, arms aggressively wrapping around me, preventing me from attacking.

I respond viscerally, struggling against the force holding me back, desperate to make him bleed some more.

"Nope, you're done. We're getting you out of here." Seth's harsh voice sounds behind me, but I continue to fight to get back to Bradshaw, his words ringing in my ears.

Mia suddenly steps in front of me and a wave of awareness crashes into me.

"We're going home now, Ethan." There is a resoluteness to her tone that is mirrored in her expression. "So, calm the fuck down."

My body sags as the adrenaline dissipates and I allow myself to be led away. One last glance back shows me Bradshaw standing tall, blood dripping down his chin and a vicious glint in his eye.

And when I see him mouth the words, "This is going to be fun" it takes all of Seth's strength to hold me back.

§

My jaw clenches at my father's low muttered curses. He's directing them at the fumbled football on the television, but we both know it's his disappointment in me that has him so on edge.

I take a drink of my cola in an effort to calm the tension that has me wound so tightly, and I wonder, not for the first time, how old I'll have to be before the idea of failing him stops tearing me up.

"What were you fucking thinking? How many times have I told you how important team unity is?" I'm not at all surprised by his outburst and when I force myself to look at him, his face is harsh, jaw tight and brows furrowed. I cringe internally. "You're lucky as fuck I was able to pull some strings and get you on the team after this asinine decision to transfer back, and you thank me by punching your captain. I mean, *fuck*, Ethan."

I don't bother reminding him that I never asked him to pull any strings. That I don't care about playing ball. Not the way he does, anyway, but I remind myself what a disappointment it must be for the former captain of the Giants to have his only son not want to follow in his footsteps.

"I had my reasons." I run a hand over my jaw and consider when I last shaved.

"You had your *reasons*? Your reasons mean shit out on the field, son."

"Ooooh, Daddy said a bad word!" I note the immediate change in atmosphere as my kid sister, Emmerson, comes running into the room. My father's back straightens and a wide smile appears as she berates him the way only a seven-year-old can.

I wonder, idly, what it's like to be loved like that. Free from the suffocation of any expectation.

"Ethan, are you staying for dinner? I got a new princess doll I wanna show you."

"I'm not sure, Oops. Why don't you show it to me now, just in case."

She folds her arms across her chest and tilts her chin up at me, glowering defiantly. "Mommy said you're not supposed to call me that!"

"Yes, she did." My mother walks along the hallway, pausing in the doorway of the heatre room, a grocery bag in each hand and a wry smile on her face. "Ethan James Miller, do not tease your sister, please. Emme, go wash your hands and we'll make a start on that pie."

Emme pokes her tongue out at me and rushes out of the room, a flurry of awkward limbs and long blonde hair.

"You know, you keep ribbing her about being an oops baby, and I'm going to tell her how you had the biggest head of any baby I've ever seen, kiddo. And you should stay for dinner." Her smile slips slightly. "We've missed you."

I nod, shortly. "Yeah, okay."

"Good. I'm ordering pizza, so it won't be long." My father and I both chuckle; my mother's legendary hatred for cooking is a long-running joke.

"Aren't returning sons supposed to get home-cooked meals? I'm feeling ripped off here."

"Is it not enough that I have to suffer through baking this pie? That Cassidy Jensen has a lot to answer for, telling Emme that she can eat dessert whenever she wants if she becomes a baker. Now, all she wants to do is bake constantly." Her lips purse in mock exasperation.

The mention of Layla's sister quickly brings my thoughts crashing back to my altercation with Bradshaw. Before I can get lost in my thoughts, my mother's sigh draws my attention. "Okay, if you haven't heard from me in an hour, send help. And by help, I mean run to the bakery and don't come back empty-handed."

My parents exchange a smile before Mom leaves the room, sighing dramatically.

'So, what are these *reasons?*"

I contemplate trying to feed him some bullshit line,

but in the end, I just decide on blunt honesty. "He was saying shit about Layla."

There's not a shred of regret in my tone and I watch my father's face intently, ready to defend myself.

He scrubs his hands up and down his face and looks at me tiredly. "When you love someone, they become your weakness." I feel my eyes widen at his words. "Oh, for fuck's sake, don't look so surprised. You've loved that girl since the day you met her. The only person who doesn't know it is her." He shakes his head with a small laugh. "You need to understand that assholes will always use that against you, and you need to be able to walk away. Trust me, no woman of worth is going to admire you for beating the shit out of someone. I learned that the hard way with your mother. You need to fight this guy with your smarts. Prove to Layla who the better man is. Outwit, outplay, outlast, and you'll get the girl."

The room is completely silent as I consider his words. "You know that's the *Survivor* tagline, right?"

"Shut up, smartass, it works here, too."

I laugh loudly at his expression of righteous indignation.

We settle back, watching the game but I can't keep my mind on it.

"You know, I remember when I told you I was going to Washington, you said that was an asinine decision."

"I did, and it was."

"If you think that, then why do you say coming home was a mistake?"

"I didn't say it was a mistake, I said it was also an asinine decision."

I roll my shoulders in frustration. "You're going to have to explain that, 'cause I don't see the difference."

"Coming home wasn't a mistake, but choosing to do it now, in your final year of college was a ridiculous decision. All you had to do was wait one more year and coming home to her would have been an easy transition. Instead, you threw your entire life into chaos."

"I couldn't wait another year, Dad." My voice is quiet but forceful.

"Well, maybe you should've considered the consequences a bit more before you ran away from your problems, instead of facing them like a man." He sighs resignedly. "I just hope all the craziness doesn't affect you on the field."

I suppress the urge to groan and am about to give him shit for being worse than a stage mom, when my phone vibrates.

Seth: Bradshaw is at Hound Dog and Layla just walked in

Seth: Get your ass down here

My fingers clench the phone to the point of pain, and I turn, prepared to make up an excuse to leave.

"Go. I'll explain to your mom and Emme." He shoos me away.

I jump up and race for the door when Dad's voice stops me in my tracks.

"Be smarter, Ethan. Be the man she deserves, not the asshole she regrets."

CHAPTER SEVEN

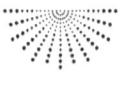

LAYLA

*M*ichael Bradshaw is talking to me. We're gathered around a table, tucked away in a quiet corner of *Hound Dog*, and he is literally ignoring everyone else, showering me with his undivided attention. It's weird, and I don't feel emotionally equipped to handle it. The only guy that has ever been so resolutely focused on me before, is Ethan, and for the life of me I can't figure out why the two feel so different.

I love Ethan's eyes on me. The way he listens to every word I say as though it's important for him to know what I'm thinking. The smile he has that is only mine.

Ethan's attention makes me feel strong, like I'm necessary. But, the last hour with Michael has only heightened my feeling of self-consciousness and with every passing second, I can feel the prickles of insecurity intensify.

"...after we won the championship things got a little crazy, but they've settled down now. We need to get our focus back if we want to make it back to back." He winks at me slyly. "And we will make it back to back."

His words grab my attention and I grimace slightly. I'm sure his comment is merely a captain with complete faith in his team, but it comes across as arrogant and irritates me.

"You must be excited to have Ethan on the team this year. He's an amazing running back." I notice a flicker of emotion crosses his face, but it's gone before I can identify it.

"He's okay. I'm not sure how long it's been since you last saw him play, but he's lucky he got a spot on the team. His old man had to pull a shitload of strings to make it happen. I'll be surprised if he makes it off the bench this season." He shrugs casually.

My eyebrows raise in surprise. While I haven't seen him play since high school, Ethan was always an instinctual player, with a natural ability to read the play. His only flaw was that he really didn't care about football, and while he would never admit it to anyone else, I knew the only reason he played was out of loyalty to his father. My stomach hurt a little at the idea of Ethan losing the little bit of joy he got from football.

"Well, speak of the fucking devil."

My eyes follow the direction of Michael's and I feel my body relax at the sight of Ethan walking through the door, his face tense as he looks around the room.

Spotting us, he walks over, his long legs making the trip much quicker than it should have been.

Standing at the end of the table, he glares down at

Michael and grabs a chair from the table opposite us, wordlessly situating himself at the end of the table, in between Michael and myself.

"Miller! Glad you could make it, man." Seth leans over past Evie and me, to do some kind of hand slap thing that has Ethan shaking his head.

Looking directly at Michael, he replies, "Wouldn't miss it." His expression is menacing and a shiver of unexplained dread travels down my spine. "Your jaw's looking better."

Michael's eyes narrow and flit to me briefly, before he exhales a slow steadying breath. I examine his jaw again, the bruising that he explained away earlier as a training accident, suddenly not looking quite so innocent.

"Yeah, the guy that got me needs to strengthen up a bit, so the damage was pretty insignificant." Before Ethan can reply, he directs his attention back to me and I drag my gaze away from Ethan to meet his.

"Hey, I have to head out but are you free Saturday night? We could get some dinner, maybe see a movie?"

He's looking at me so sincerely, and at the same time, I can feel Ethan's penetrating stare causing me to feel completely torn. I have no idea what is going on between these two, but if I want to have Ethan in my life, then I need to move on and stop pining for him.

Ignoring Ethan, I slap on what I hope is a convincing smile and nod.

"Sure, I'd love to." We spend the next few minutes exchanging numbers before Michael loudly farewells the group. All the while I feel Ethan glowering at me.

"What?!" I finally snap, my frustration peaking.

"The guy's an asshole. You should stay away from him."

"Well, he's never been anything but nice to me, so maybe you should keep your opinions to yourself." Anger is emanating from Ethan forcefully, and I'm shocked by its vehemence.

"Did he even know your name a week ago? Before he realized he could get to me through you?"

My head snaps back and I feel as though I've been slapped.

"Why? Because that's the only reason a guy like that could be interested in me?"

He stares back at me, his face like granite, aggressively unapologetic.

"Yes."

One word. Who would have thought that one word was all it took to shatter a person?

I feel the burn of tears, but I refuse to let them fall, so I sit there mutely, unsure how to respond to his cruelness.

"You asshole." Evie's voice quietly seethes next to me. "I can't believe I was Team Ethan. You can go fuck yourself." She starts to push me into motion. "C'mon, Lay, move. Let's get out of here."

"Wait, what?" Every drop of anger has fallen from Ethan's face as he watches us in confusion.

"Stop." He places a hand on my arm to still me. "*Wait.*"

He looks ashen and I can see the reality of what he said settle. "I didn't mean it like that.

"How the hell else could you mean it, douchebag?" His eyes cut between Evie and me, a look of anxiety blanketed over his face before his eyes settle on me.

"Guys like that aren't interested in girls like you, Bug. He wants the easy fuck. The girl that will blow him and then move on to the next guy as soon as she's swallowed. He's not looking for a girlfriend, just a fuck buddy. And that's not what you are."

I tense at his crudeness, watching closely as his hand reaches up and grips his neck, kneading the skin, knowing it's a nervous tic of his.

"Christ, Layla, I didn't mean that you weren't good enough for him. You're *too* fucking good."

I lean back in my seat and attempt to let the emotions of the last few minutes settle, but I'm getting lost in my head, allowing negative emotions to drag me under.

I feel his hand take mine, his fingers threading through my own, and immediately a sense of calm envelops me. Nobody soothes me the way he does. I've missed it.

Looking up, I note, thankfully, that our little confrontation has gone unnoticed by those around us. They are too distracted by Seth and Mia, telling a story in their own unique way. One that involves a lot of arguing, much to the amusement of the rest of the group.

Evie's sitting quietly next to me, the fight gone, considering Ethan thoughtfully.

"Just be careful, Layla, please? I don't trust him." He bites down on his bottom lip, and my eyes zero in on the action, distracting me. "That guy only cares about himself, and I don't want you to get hurt. Just promise me you'll think about what I'm saying."

I focus on our hands, still entwined, and the way Ethan slides his thumb along my skin. Small teasing strokes that I could so easily read too much into.

"There you are. I've been looking all over for you!" The spell broken, I glance up and see Tash standing next to Ethan, her words directed at Evie and me, but her eyes locked steadfastly on Ethan's profile.

She takes the seat that Michael vacated, and I can't help the ominous feeling that everything is about to change, no matter how hard I fight it.

&

"Need a hand?"

"Oh!" My hand flies to my chest in a desperate attempt to steady my heartbeat. "Don't *do* that!"

Skye laughs softly at my reaction. "Sorry, I thought you saw me coming. You want me to help with these books? Cass will be here soon, won't she?"

"Yep, that would be great, thanks." Skye takes the spot next to me and we get to work shelving the new stock that arrived at *Books & Beans* this morning.

Working in tandem, we silently get through the large pile, stepping up on our tippy toes to reach the higher shelves and exchanging looks that only a fellow shorty would understand, every time.

We have almost finished the job when Skye breaks the silence with a gentle clearing of her throat.

"So, Cassidy mentioned she hasn't seen much of you lately. Everything going okay?"

Now, I should mention that I love having Skye as my boss. She's fair and understanding, and pretty much exactly what everyone wants in a boss. But, occasionally, there are times when having a boss who has known me since I was a tubby eleven-year-old and is best friends with my big sister, can be a pain in the behind.

"Yeah, everything's great. Just busy, you know?" I cringe inwardly and pray my attempt at flippancy has worked.

Skye places the last book on the shelf to her left and then turns to face me, her eyes narrowing so slightly, that most people wouldn't even notice. "Okay, I know how busy college can be, especially your last year."

I force a smile and begin to move away when she grabs my arm, stopping me.

"But if anything is going on, you can talk to me. I know how full-on Cassidy can be, and I know sometimes she reacts without thinking. I'm here if you need me. I just need you to know that."

Without thinking, I throw my arms around her, getting a face full of her long, wavy brown hair and mutter a quiet thank you.

Pulling back, she strokes a hand over my cheek, smiling softly. "Anytime, Lay."

I begin to push the trolley we use to move the boxes of books through the store toward the stockroom when Skye calls out again. "You'll be back by two?

Juliet has an appointment with her lawyer at two-thirty, and she wants me there for some reason."

A smile lights up my face at the mention of Juliet, the owner of *Books & Beans*. She retired recently, leaving Skye to manage the place, and as happy as I am for Skye, I do miss her. She was like a doting aunt, who was always there with a listening ear, homemade shortbread and sometimes inappropriate advice.

"Yeah, I'll definitely be back by then, no worries."

I make my way to the stockroom, getting lost in my head as I consider what Skye said about Cassidy.

I love my sister. Actually, I adore her. There's not much not to love. She's loud, confident and she loves with her entire heart. She's also stunningly beautiful. With the exception of our blonde hair, we look nothing alike and are actually complete opposites.

She's tall to my short. She's cerulean blue eyes to my murky brown. She's beautiful to my plain. And no matter how much I love her, spending a lifetime being compared, and falling very short, leaves me feeling even more self-conscious than normal when I'm around her. No matter how hard I try to fight it.

Shaking my head in frustration, I decide that today I am going to get over myself and enjoy my time with Cassidy. Putting all the equipment back where it belongs, I straighten my back and stride determinedly toward the counter that has my purse underneath but as I glance up toward the door, all air forcefully leaves my body, leaving me breathless at the sight headed my way.

CHAPTER EIGHT

ETHAN

She looks beautiful. Stunned and slightly murderous, but still beautiful as fuck.

Twisting my head, I lean down slightly to whisper in Cassidy's ear. "She doesn't look too happy to see me."

Cassidy wrinkles her nose in disgust at my words. "Who the fuck cares? Jesus, if I had a dollar for every time someone looked at me like that, I'd have my bakery by now." She squeezes my forearm roughly, reminding me of the unpleasant greeting I received earlier, my cheek stinging at the memory. "Suck it up, buttercup. You deserve for her to cut your dick off after the way you ghosted her. Now smile real pretty, so I don't regret letting you tag along, 'kay?"

Nodding, we stop abruptly when Layla stands right in front of us.

"What's going on here?" She quirks a brow at her sister in challenge.

"You ready to go?" Cassidy ignores her question

entirely, instead looping her arm through Layla's and taking off, leaving me behind. "You coming, Hollywood?" she throws over her shoulder.

Layla snorts out a laugh, and I grimace, glaring at Cassidy. She has an awful habit of nicknaming everyone and when you get stuck with the bullshit name *Hollywood* at thirteen, well, let's just say that's tough for a guy to live down.

"C'mon, *Millhouse*, I've only got an hour, so hurry up." Layla smirks at me.

Jesus, these fucking two.

Ten minutes later I'm being dragged into a bakery that boasts *'The best high tea in New York,'* and Layla describes as "oh my God, how quaint!" while I wonder what the fuck I'm doing.

"What the hell is high tea?" A thought crosses my mind. "Does it involve pot brownies? 'Cause Coach would kill me if he ever found out."

Layla giggles and Cassidy snorts at my question.

"It's a fancy schmancy afternoon tea, dipwad, and it's very classy. Think posh English people eating tiny sandwiches and cakes. I'm considering offering it as a new service to my clients," Cassidy explains.

After getting settled and ordering what is essentially a snack for me, I begin mentally planning my second lunch while the girls launch into a stream of meaningless chit-chat, catching up on all the gossip, and completely ignoring me.

My phone pings and I glance at it in annoyance when I see Tash's name appear on the screen. I have no idea who gave her my number, but they're going to cop it when I find out. The chick has been annoying me all week and can't seem to take the hint that I'm not interested.

I sit silently, listening to the girls talk and biting my tongue in an attempt not to bring up Bradshaw and Layla's date tonight. But really, it's the *only* thing I want to talk about.

"So, I want to experiment with some new flavors tonight, bubs, you wanna be my guinea pig? I'll even sweeten the deal with *The Greatest Showman*, and we can spend the night drooling over cupcakes and Zac Efron." Cassidy's question grabs my attention and I seize my opportunity like the ultimate running back I am.

"She can't. She has a date."

"Are you fucking kidding me?!"

The waitress picks this moment to arrive with our cute – Layla's words, not mine – lunch and she flushes with embarrassment at her sister's outburst.

Luckily the server's only response is a small smile as she places the tiered rack, holding a variety of sandwiches – with their fucking crusts cut off – and tiny cakes and pastries. I swear to God, if there are cucumber sandwiches on that thing, I'm walking out in disgust.

"Bubs! Why didn't you tell me you had a date? It's been ages since that last fuckwad. It's about freaking time."

My ears perk up. "What fuckwad?"

Cassidy waves me off like an annoying gnat. "Just some loser who didn't know amazing when he had it."

"CJ, shut up," Layla hisses, and I make a mental note to find out more about this guy, who I instinctively want to hurt, later.

"Christ, fine." Cassidy side-eyes me while taking her pick of the miniature sandwiches. My eyes narrow as she adds a third one to her plate, leaving only... four, five, six, *six* left. Fuck, I'm going to starve.

"Okay, you're up, Hollywood, tell me everything she won't."

All thoughts of starving, forgotten, I answer honestly. "He's a dickhead, and she shouldn't be wasting her time with him."

She sighs dramatically, which is pretty much how Cassidy does everything. "And that's your completely unbiased opinion, I suppose?"

Layla chooses this moment to interrupt, and her answer has me clenching my jaw.

"No, it's not unbiased." She glares at me across the table. "They hate each other for some reason, and that's what he's basing his opinion on."

"Don't you trust that I have my reasons for hating him?"

"Well, then shouldn't I consider that he hates you? Maybe I shouldn't have been so quick to forgive you?"

"Forgive me? It doesn't feel like you've forgiven me." I can't help the edge of bitterness in my voice. "We used to talk every day. I barely see you now." I let the resentment flow through me, and for the first time, I acknowledge that I'm pissed. That even though I was the asshole who ruined our friendship, she said we could start over and she hasn't put any effort into reconnecting.

"Are you kidding me right now, Ethan?"

But I meet her stare resolutely, determined not to back down.

A plate scraping across the table reminds us that we're not alone and we both turn toward Cassidy, who is munching on a pitiful sandwich, eyes wide, swinging her gaze between the two of us.

"Oh, don't mind me, I'm just here for the comments and all that jazz. You guys go on."

Layla shakes her head in annoyance before facing me. I try my best to keep a stoic face on but fuck it. I turned my life upside down to fix things with her, and she said she would try. And it's fucking killing me that she keeps holding me at arm's length. Fuck Seth and his "maybe something can happen" bullshit. At this point, I'll settle for having my best friend back.

Her face softens as she looks at me, and I can breathe a little bit easier. This is my Layla.

"I'm sorry if I've made you feel that way." She sighs a sigh so deep, I can almost see her body vibrate. "I'm trying, I promise I am. I just… I don't know. I'm trying. That's all I can tell you."

"It doesn't feel like you're trying when you ignore my messages," I mutter. I sound like a pouting child, and I could happily bitch slap my whiny ass right now.

"Oh, my fucking God," Cassidy butts in, her voice loaded with exasperation. "Layla, do you promise to answer Ethan's messages from now on?" She nods.

"Good. Ethan, do you promise not to be a complete douchehole and disappear from Layla's life again?"

"Yes."

"Okay, then. I now pronounce your petty asses BFFs again," she huffs, grabbing another sandwich. "Now, can we talk about something more important? Like my annoying, pain-in-the-ass boss? Do you know what Sunshine did to me yesterday?"

She then launches into a forty-five-minute tirade that has me pitying her unsuspecting boss.

I never did get any food.

&

Later that afternoon, I've got my ass planted on the sofa, ESPN on the TV and I'm chowing down on some mac and cheese when Mia comes storming in.

"I'm going to kill him!"

This statement should worry me. Or at the very least, cause my eyes to leave the television screen. It does neither.

You see, Seth and Mia have this strange kind of love/hate, fight/fuck relationship. But it seems to work for them, and I've given up trying to figure it out.

"Do you know what he did? Do you have any idea what that idiot did?"

I continue eating, smart enough to realize that my input in this conversation is completely unnecessary.

"He got a life-size cardboard cut-out of himself made. Naked, mind you. *Naked!* Holding a picture of me, *me*, in front of his tiny little dick, and left it in the dorm's bathroom. Everyone saw it. Everyone! Now, they all think I'm dating an insane person." She flops down on the recliner across the room. "I should cut his dick off, that's what I should do."

It's this comment, said in a malicious whisper, that finally gets my attention.

"Please, don't. I don't need that kind of drama in my life," I respond wryly.

She's staring off into space, a glazed expression on her face, and I watch her unabashedly, wondering if she's fantasizing about Seth's death and just how painful she's planning on making it.

"Ugh, I won't. His dick is actually huge and he's really good with it, so I would just be punishing myself."

I choke on my mac and cheese and grab for my water on the coffee table as my eyes tear up. After swallowing half the bottle down, I gasp for air before hitting Mia with my most ball-busting glare. "Don't ever, and I mean *ever*, talk about one guy's dick to another guy. Jesus, I could've choked!"

She snorts out a laugh. "Funny, I said exactly the same thing last night."

I groan loudly, and she cackles as I try to erase the unwanted images of her deepthroating Seth from my mind. Someone pass the fucking eye bleach.

"What have you got planned for tonight?"

My mouth pulls down in a frown, her question reminding me of Layla and Bradshaw's date.

"Nothing," I reply sulkily.

"Want to come out with us? We're going to check out Trent's birthday party."

"You make it sound like a ten-year-old's party," I scoff.

"Well, excuse me, douchebag. Consider the offer rescinded."

I cringe at her tone and hate myself a little more for being so rude to her.

"Sorry. I'm just not up for going out tonight."

She looks at me curiously. "This have something to do with Layla?"

A scowl falls across my face at her question. "She's going out with Bradshaw tonight."

Mia jumps up excitedly, rushing over to take a seat on the sofa beside me, her legs curled underneath her, and blatant interest scrawled over her face. "So, what's the deal with you two? Like, did you used to date and now you're trying the friends thing? 'Cause there's definitely a vibe between you."

"Nope, never dated, best friends who lost touch for a while, that's it."

Her eyes zero in on me suspiciously. "Nuh-uh, not buying it. You two have the zing."

"The zing?" I sneer. "What the hell is the zing?"

Mia sighs loudly and looks at me as though she hasn't had to deal with this level of stupid before. "The *zing* is when you can tell that two people want to rip each other's clothes off, just by looking at them. It's chemistry, Ethan, and you two? You've got it."

I lean forward, place my empty bowl on the coffee table and turn my body so I'm fully facing her. "Look, the thing is, I've been in love with her since the day I saw her lying in a field, crying her eyes out. I was four and I thought she was the most beautiful thing I'd ever seen. Even with puffy eyes and snot trails. But she's never felt that way about me, and I'm doing my best to be okay with that, so hearing shit like that doesn't help me." I shrug.

Mia is watching me, her brow furrowed in concern. "That's so sad." She smirks at me. "But also, completely untrue."

I shake my head and decide the only way to make her see sense is to give her the whole uncensored story. I lay out all my cards, explaining how my feelings grew over the years, how it felt seeing her never shine the way she deserved to. How many fights I got into, and threats I handed out, defending her to ignorant douches who never could see what she worked so hard to hide. I told her how hurt I was when Layla blew me off for the prom and how hard it was to watch her with someone else. I shared it all. Even my supreme assholeishness when I ghosted on her so epically.

I watched as her expression morphed from one of sympathy to one of frustration and finally anger.

When I'm finally all storied out, we sit in silence. Me, exhausted from spilling my guts and her, well, I think in disbelief.

Mia looks up at me, an unreadable expression on her face.

"So, yeah, she's never felt that way about me. If she had, I definitely would know."

A small smile teases her lips, and she shakes her

head slowly. "You poor deluded fool." She stands, stretching tall and working the kinks out of her long, lean body before walking toward the kitchen.

Pausing, she stands in the doorway, folding her arms across her chest. "You should try and see her tonight, after her date. Make sure you're the one she's thinking about when her head hits her pillow." She shakes her head again, and a gentle laugh escapes her as she walks away. "God, your grandchildren are going to love that story."

CHAPTER NINE

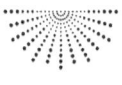

LAYLA

*E*vie tucks a stray lock of hair behind my ear, a serious look on her face before declaring, "Perfect."

I stand in front of the full-length mirror on the back of our door, taking in my reflection and wish I could muster the same enthusiasm.

"You look gorgeous, Lay. Michael's gonna come in his pants the second he sees how hot you look tonight." I grimace at her crude assessment. She sounds so assured and I envy her confidence in me.

"It'll do," I reply with a shrug. It's the best I can do.

"Ugh, whatever." Rolling her eyes, she pushes me toward the bed, sits me down and begins spraying me generously, with her favorite perfume.

I cough and wave my hands around desperately as my lungs burn each time I inhale another mouthful of toxic air.

"Enough! That's enough!" She looks at me innocently before replacing the cap and putting the bottle away.

"Are you nervous?"

Her question rattles me. I had gone to my happy place where nerves can't reach me, a subtle numbness enveloping me, but her question drags me back to reality and forces me to consider what I'm about to do.

"Do you think he was right?"

Evie's face pinches in confusion. "Do I think who was right about what?"

"Ethan. Do you think he was right when he said Michael's only trying to get to him by dating me?"

"Okay, let me start this by saying that I am Team Ethan." My eyes narrow in confusion. "Don't look at me like that. That boy is into you, and I am fully on board with Layhan becoming a thing."

"Layhan?"

She holds a finger up, effectively silencing me. "Don't interrupt. But until you both pull your heads out of your asses and make that happen, I'm all for you going out and having fun. And maybe Michael did only notice you because of Ethan, because God knows you're not out there flaunting your wares for all the guys to see, but do I think he's dating you just to piss Ethan off? No, I don't." She takes a deep breath before continuing with a mischievous smirk. "That's just an added bonus."

Her little speech has thoroughly confused me, so I grasp onto the completely ridiculous.

"Layhan?"

A knock on the door saves Evie from answering, and she practically falls over herself to get to it. Before turning the doorknob, she turns to me and mouths, "You ready?" I stand up and nod, my brain still not fully caught up after her spiel.

Michael steps into our room and his eyes widen slightly as he takes me in.

I self-consciously smooth my hands down my black sweater dress that ends mid-thigh and hugs my many curves in a way I'm not entirely comfortable with.

"You look incredible, Layla." He smiles at me appreciatively, and I feel a little bit of my anxiety melt away. "You ready to go?"

I smile with more confidence than I'm feeling and reach out to take his proffered hand.

"Let's do this."

❧

Belladonna is fancy. Much fancier than I'm used to, but I can't deny the elegant restaurant has a warmth that evokes romance and intimacy. The ideal place for both a first date or a twenty-year anniversary dinner, it really is perfect.

"This place is beautiful." My voice holds a note of reverence and I can't stop my eyes bouncing around, trying to take everything in.

"Yeah, my sister recommended it, it's her favorite restaurant."

My face warms at the idea of him going to his sister

about our date. "Well, color me impressed. Although, I am surprised you had to get tips from your sister. I would've thought you would know all the best places to impress the girls."

"Meh, I don't date much." He cringes slightly when he realizes what he just said. I smile brightly in an attempt to put his mind at ease. His slut status is well known on campus, but I'm not one to shame a person, so long as they're not hurting anybody.

"Calm down, cowboy, I choose to be flattered by that statement." I snort.

He eyes me curiously. "You know, you're not what I expected."

I immediately tamp down my inner voice. She's a nasty witch and I'm trying to learn to ignore her.

"Thanks?" I question drolly.

"No, shit, sorry. I just mean, you seem so quiet and you kinda keep to yourself. I don't think you had ever actually looked at me before that morning in the coffee shop. I guess I kind of thought you might be a bit stuck up?"

I unconsciously flinch at his observation. It's not the first time I've heard it, but it still stings, and I can't help the wave of shame that washes over me. Nobody wants people to think they're an uppity snob.

"I'm shy, that's all. It's hard for me to get to know people." I try to keep my voice from shaking.

"You seem to know Miller pretty well." He's arching a brow at me, but there's no antagonism there, only playful curiosity, and I relax slightly.

"I've known Ethan practically my whole life." Now

it's my turn to challenge him. "Is that the only reason you asked me out? To annoy him?"

Michael has the good grace to duck his head in embarrassment.

"Honestly? That was the plan. He was giving off all kinds of fuck off vibes that morning in the coffee shop, and I don't like him, so I figured flirting with you would be an easy way to piss him off." He pauses briefly and my inner voice slash witch, starts to whisper, *'I told you so.'*

"But that night at *Hound Dog*, you were different. Watching you with your friend and Miller, you were funny and relaxed." He shrugs. "You seemed like someone I wanted to get to know. Pissing Miller off is just the icing on the cake. Scout's honor." He holds his right hand up in the universal sign, a slow smile spreading across his face.

I consider what he said and realize that I'm not entirely surprised and I think I can live with his explanation.

"Plus, you're hot as fuck and that's always good for the rep." He winks at me across the table, and I groan before we both dissolve into laughter.

Maybe tonight will be more fun than I had expected.

"I just can't believe that ending." I shake my head, still reeling from the surprise ending of the movie.

Michael chuckles beside me, his warm hand

holding mine as we stroll across campus, making our way back to my dorm.

"I still can't believe you wanted to see *Infinity War*. I was all set to suffer through some cheesy rom-com."

The leaves crunch beneath our feet and the sight of my breath puffing out in a small cloud highlights the chill in the air. I can feel the flush in my cheeks, but despite all of this, there is a warmth spreading through me at the memory of tonight's date and how well it has gone.

Michael one-on-one isn't nearly as overwhelming as he is in a group of his fawning groupies. He's actually quite charming and endearing, in a boyish kind of way.

"I'm going to pretend you didn't say that," I scoff. "Plenty of girls love those movies." I pause briefly. "But I do love a good rom-com too."

He holds his hands up in surrender. "Fair enough, I can admit when I'm wrong." He huffs out a laugh and a shiver races up my spine. Mistaking it for a chill, Michael releases my hand, throwing his arm around me and pulling me in close to him. His body heat immediately warms me, but also fills me with a slight sense of discomfort that I'm at a loss to explain.

Two minutes ago, his laugh was giving me the shivers, so why does his touch feel so wrong?

I spend the remainder of our short walk trying to get out of my head and focus on enjoying Michael's company.

Coming to a stop in front of my building, he turns and pulls my body close to his.

"I had a great time tonight." A small smile plays on his lips, and my breath hitches as I realize that I have no desire to kiss him. Ridiculously, I feel the burn of tears as I try to figure out why, only a month ago the thought of kissing him made my pulse race, and my thighs clench, but right now? It just fills me with dread.

Giving myself a mental shake, I pull myself together enough to respond.

"I did, too." I force a smile and pray he can't see right through me.

Turns out he can't because the next thing I know, he is leaning down and brushing a kiss across my lips. His mouth moves against mine, sweetly, definitely not what I expected from a Michael Bradshaw kiss, and despite my hesitation, I find myself responding. With my eyes closed, I allow myself to fall into the kiss and press my body closer to his, as Ethan's hands – wait, what?

My eyes snap open and I pull back in shock to find Michael, *not Ethan*, staring down at me, a hint of confusion in his expression.

My cheeks flush, this time in embarrassment rather than with a chill, and I take a step away from him. His arms fall to his side, but he rallies quickly.

"I'll call you?"

I nod slightly. "Sure." I try to sound enthusiastic, but my head is too confused to fake it. Doing my best to appear unaffected, I throw him a smile and turn toward my dorm.

My mind is racing as I make my way back to my room. I consider myself pretty self-aware and I know

I'm not over Ethan. But I also know I've been crushing on Michael Bradshaw for months. So, why can't my heart let me enjoy the guy who *is* interested in me, rather than pine over the guy I can never have?

Sighing, I push my door open and gasp in shock.

CHAPTER TEN

ETHAN

"*H*ey, Bug, how's it going?"

Her eyes practically pop out of her head before skimming their way along my body, which is casually reclined on her bed, her laptop propped on my knees, an old episode of *The Office* playing.

Her shoulders sag slightly in defeat and she makes her way toward the bed, silently.

"Move over." She attempts to push me aside, but considering I have a foot and a hundred pounds on her, she fails miserably. Being the gentleman I am, I scoot over, making enough room for her to lie down.

"You should stop calling me that, you know."

"What? Bug?" Like fuck, I'll stop. "Why?"

"It makes me sound like a five-year-old," she replies sulkily, and I have to fight back a laugh.

"Give me your phone."

"Why?" Her voice is laced with suspicion, but I ignore it, holding out a hand impatiently.

"Just hand it over."

"Ugh, fine. *Here.*" She thrusts her phone at me, and I bite my lip, willing my body not to react to her pouty expression.

I quickly pull up her lock screen and fight back an exclamation of triumph when I see it. A close-up picture of two ladybugs, crawling along the stem of a beautiful wildflower. She has been obsessed with ladybugs since we were kids and was constantly dragging me through the field behind her house, searching for them.

I have so many memories connected to those tiny-ass ladybugs, so, no. I will never stop calling her Bug. No matter how sexy she looks, pouting at me like that.

"Never gonna happen." I hand her phone back and turn my attention back to the laptop. It's the Christmas episode when Jim has bought Pam a teapot and filled it with surprises, including a note confessing his feelings. But his plan to give it to her is thwarted when Steve Carell's character insists on playing "Yankee Swap" instead of sticking to Secret Santa.

Layla reaches out to move the screen slightly, and then curls into my side, her head on my shoulder. I can't remember how many times we lay like this over the years, but I do remember it stopped abruptly the night my dick could no longer control itself when a half-asleep Layla pressed her body into mine, a little too intimately.

"You know, I have no idea how Pam was so clueless. It's so obvious Jim's in love with her and they're perfect for each other. What's she thinking wasting her time with Roy?"

I want to laugh at the irony of this but can't quite manage it. Instead, I nod noncommittally.

"So, how was your date tonight?" I do my best to sound unbothered, but Layla knows me too well and turns slightly, giving me the side-eye.

"Really? You really want to talk about my date, or do you just want an excuse to moan about Michael?"

I close my eyes and squeeze them shut for a moment. *Friendship,* I tell myself. *Don't be an asshole, she's your friend, be supportive.*

"Yes, I want to know how it went," I force out. "I promise to overlook his douchiness and be a supportive friend."

She groans loudly, and my dick twitches at the sound. Jesus, I need to get that under control quickly.

"You're a pain in the butt, you know that?" She slaps me playfully on the chest. "Okay, well, it was good, I guess. He took me to a great restaurant; the food was awesome, and then we went and saw the new Avengers movie. It was fun."

I suppress a grimace. "That's good."

Her laugh fills the room, and I know without a shadow of a doubt that this friends thing is going to be the hardest thing I've ever done. Because damn if the sound of her laughter doesn't have my cock hardening.

"That was the least convincing 'that's good' I've ever heard."

"It *is* good. I'm not an asshole, Lay. I want you to be happy." I can't help adding, "Even if I have no idea how *he* could make you happy."

She snorts, and fuck, I've missed that sound. "You

never did like any guy I dated, so I actually think you're doing well, considering how much you hate him." She rolls over onto her side, so she's facing me. "Why exactly do you hate him so much?"

I debate how to answer her question honestly, remembering every time Bradshaw has bragged about all the pussy he pounds. How he cruelly belittles the girls who sleep with him to a locker room full of horny jocks, offering up their phone numbers, as well as disgusting commentary on their sexual abilities, like some kind of prize.

In an attempt to appear impartial, I offer a casual, "Just a personality clash, I guess," while already planning how I'll kill the motherfucker if I ever hear him talk about Layla like that.

"What about you?"

Her question throws me. "What about me, what?"

"What about you and girls? Are you seeing anyone? What have I missed?"

My stomach drops at the idea of telling her about the insanity of my first year at college. How I tried to fuck her out of my system with any willing girl. The desperation I felt when all that did was exacerbate the problem, leaving me feeling empty and pathetically alone.

Making a conscious decision to leave that information in the past, where it belongs, I give her the censored version.

"Nothing serious. I dated a few girls, but nothing took. I'm still looking for my Pam, I guess."

At the sound of my words, her eyes flick back to the

screen and she slaps my stomach, her hand a little too close to my waistband for my comfort.

"This bit makes me so sad." I follow her gaze to the laptop screen where Jim is finally giving Pam her teapot, but he covertly sneaks his love note into his pocket.

"Ugh, why doesn't he just tell her? It's *so* frustrating!"

"You don't think it would be terrifying to tell your best friend you love them?" The question has left my mouth before I even realize the thought.

"Oh God, no, in real life you should never do it. That's a sure-fire way to ruin a friendship. But this is television, so, yes, Jim should totally sac up and declare his love."

And if I ever wondered if Layla and I could possibly ever happen, I have my answer.

The noise of the locker room is suffocating and that combined with the number of dicks flying around today, I can't wait to get out of the building.

"How fucking cool was that?" Seth exclaims. "Using your dick as a puppet? Fucking genius!"

"I don't even want to think about what Taylor was searching for when he discovered that video." Referring to the YouTube video of a couple of Australian guys who do a puppet show with their dicks, I shake my head and snicker. "I don't know whether to be impressed or concerned by their ingenuity." I use my shoulder to give him a shove. "I do know that I could have done without all you assholes trying to copy their moves. I'm pretty sure I'm scarred for life after seeing that."

"Dude, you loved it, I know you're always looking for an excuse to see my junk."

"Not even your girlfriend wants to see your junk, man, maybe you should start keeping it in your pants. Keep some mystery."

"Whatever, Miller." He leans over and plants a sloppy kiss on my cheek. "Catch ya later."

Christ, why the hell am I friends with him? Right, he had a spare room to rent. Although, with his lack of boundaries, it's becoming clear why he goes through so many roommates.

"Ethan?"

I look over my shoulder to the small voice that's calling my name and try to hide my annoyance when I see Tash walking toward me.

"Hey, Tash. What's up?"

She falls into step beside me and when she matches my strides, I notice for the first time, how tall she is. Risking a sideways glance, I admire her long, toned legs, but immediately kick myself when she catches me, laughing lightly, and slips her arm through mine, holding on tight.

"Go ahead and look. I have great legs, they deserve to be admired." She giggles, but I can't help thinking it feels rehearsed and it sucks away the tiny granule of respect I felt for her confidence.

Coughing, I look away. "Did you want something?"

"Yes. Are you ready to agree to a date, yet? I heard Layla say you wanted to see that Chris Evans movie, and I'm psyched to see it, too." She arches a perfect brow at me. "You *up* for it?"

I choose to ignore her innuendo, instead zeroing in on the part of her sentence that actually interests me.

"Layla was talking about me?" Jesus, I hope I don't sound like as much of a pussy as I think I do.

Tash stops in her tracks, our arms still entwined so I'm pulled backward, and she stares at me incredulously. Okay, yeah, I guess you can call me Pussy Boy.

"What?" My voice is rough with embarrassment. This chick is the last person I want to know about my feelings for Layla.

Shaking her head, she smirks at me and I get the distinct impression that Tash has a conniving side she would have no problem utilizing if needed. And I'm not going to lie. That makes me nervous as fuck.

"Nothing, nothing at all." She laughs. "Okay, so I'm guessing a date is out of the question, then. What about a fuck?"

I whip my head around, eyes wide and pretty much choke on my own spit as her words sink in.

She laughs again, a slightly mocking snigger that causes my hackles to rise.

"Fuck, Ethan. We should fuck." She sighs dramatically. "Look, I get that you're into Layla." I start to argue, but she barrels on. "I mean I'm not going to lie, I don't get it. She's very sweet, but she's kinda blah if you ask me."

Those hackles that had risen? They're fucking jumping in anger now.

"Jesus, aren't you supposed to be her friend? She's so fucking far from blah, and if you really knew her, you'd fucking know that." I'm beyond pissed right now, and when she throws her hands up in mock surrender and widens her eyes innocently, I'm ready to leave this bitch in the dust.

"Of course I'm her friend!" She has the nerve to chastise me. "I just want her to be the best she can be." Tash rolls her eyes and nudges me with her elbow, as though we're fucking BFFs. "She never listens to me though."

Thank Christ for that, I can't help thinking.

"Well, speak of the devil and she appears."

I ignore the hardness in Tash's tone as I look up to see Layla and Evie walking into the dining hall.

I immediately head in their direction, determined to continue the headway I made the other night. It was the closest we'd come to feeling like old times and I was intent on not backsliding.

"Hey, we're not done here, Ethan!" she calls to my retreating back. She sounds all kinds of irritated, but I can't quite bring myself to care.

"Yeah, we are."

CHAPTER ELEVEN

LAYLA

"*H*ey! Layla! Evie! Wait up!"

I look over my shoulder and see Ethan jogging our way. The start of a smile sneaks across my lips, but it stops abruptly when I notice Tash right behind him, trying to keep up with a look of annoyance plastered all over her face.

I hate the twinge of jealousy that shoots through me as I imagine them together.

I ignore the painful stab of emotion and lean into Ethan's touch as he pulls me into a side hug.

"Have either of you started that art history paper yet?" He shakes his head ruefully. "I've got to admit, I thought that class would be a cakewalk, but I'm kinda worried it's gonna kick my ass."

I give him a playful shove and laugh. Ethan has never struggled with classes, it's one of his most infuriating qualities.

"Just think of all the incredible buildings you'll

design after everything you learn in this course. You'll be the most sought-after architect in New York."

"Just New York?" he teases.

"To begin with." I nod seriously. "But then your reputation will grow and people will come from all around the world to have you design majestic buildings that they'll then brag about to all of their rich friends. Dude, you are going to be famous!" I partner my last sentence with a huge cheesy grin, remembering how much Ethan loathes the limelight.

As the son of an ESPY-award-winning, NFL Hall of Famer, he spent a lot of his childhood being paraded around as a pivotal part of his father's perfect life. And as much as he loves his dad, he found the pressure suffocating.

Rolling his eyes, he replies, "Yeah, 'cause that's my life dream."

"Oh my God, don't knock it, I would love to be famous one day," Tash interrupts, with a sigh.

Ethan's eyes connect with mine, his filled with humor, mine filled with frustration. Sometimes, I find her superficiality too much. I can overlook her condescending comments about my clothes and my hair. I understand that in her own way, she believes she's helping. But I worry that one of the reasons she's so desperate to sink her claws into Ethan is that she believes his father's celebrity status will shine a light on her. It might make me a horrible person, but he can do so much better, and if I have to suffer through seeing him with someone else, I need it to at least be someone worthy of his awesome.

A rush of warmth hits us as we make our way inside, and my stomach immediately grumbles its approval. Realizing I forgot to grab a granola bar on my way to class this morning, I thank the food gods that my college has a dining hall that can rival any food court and start visualizing my plan of attack.

The four of us split up before meeting at a large table by the side exit, slightly hidden away from the chaos.

Taking a seat next to Ethan, my eyes practically roll back in pleasure when the smell of his burger and loaded cheese fries hits my nostrils.

"Ugh, that smells so good!"

"Yep, the burgers here are fucking amazing." He eyes my plate suspiciously. "But, uh, that looks good too."

"That was convincing." I snort. Picking up my ham and salad wrap, I bite down and groan in pleasure.

"You know, there's so much fat in that, Ethan. Don't you have team nutritionists that would kick your ass for eating something like that?" Tash can't hide the disgust in her voice and her brow is laughably crinkled as she observes him devouring his burger.

Evie and I glance at each other and I have to bite my lip, *hard*, to stop my laughter from escaping.

"That's why I avoid sharing meals with our nutritionists whenever possible." He shrugs good-naturedly. "If it makes you feel better, I promise to do an extra hour of cardio tonight."

She looks down and plays with her sad-looking

garden salad. "If you say so. It's none of my business, I guess. I was just trying to look out for you."

Ethan's face echoes the surprise I'm feeling. He reaches over and gently squeezes her shoulder. "Thank you. I appreciate it."

Evie pulls a face at me and I giggle quietly before we all return to our food.

Twenty minutes later we have been joined by various members of the football team, not to mention their groupies, and I'm cursing Ethan's presence for removing my ability to remain invisible.

Keeping my attention focused on Evie and Mia, who arrived at the table mid-argument with Seth, we're having a passionate discussion about soulmates.

"I'm not saying they don't exist, I'm just saying that I don't think there's someone out there for *everyone*. I mean, that's statistically impossible, right?" I insist.

"Nope, there is totally someone out there for every-one. You might need to lower your expectations though, 'cause believe me, if you had told me Seth Parker was my soulmate five years ago, I would have laughed in your face." Her face softens. "But, he's it for me, and there's not a damn thing I can do about it." She purses her lips. "Trust me, I've tried."

Evie laughs, nodding her head in agreement. "It takes work, and sometimes you have to trust that they'll finally figure out what you already know." Her eyes cloud over, and I just know she's thinking about the guy she left behind in her small town. "But I honestly believe we all have someone that's destined to be in our lives. What sort of life is it, if it's spent without the hope of passion and intimacy?"

"I hope you're right, I really do, but I just don't think—"

"Oh my God, Layla!" Tash, who has been engaged in a low-key flirt fest with one of the football players, suddenly interrupts loudly, drawing everyone's attention.

"Jesus Christ, there are plenty of other ugly girls out there who have boyfriends, if you just—" Her voice breaks off, as though she has suddenly realized what she just said.

My vision blurs and humiliation washes over me as the meaning of Tash's words sink in around the table. Glancing up, I see embarrassed looks being exchanged and a couple of jaws hanging open. Tash, at least, has the decency to look ashamed.

"I didn't mean, I mean, just because you're—" She's stumbling over her words in an effort to save face and I take pity on her, cutting her off.

"You know what? People have all kinds of weird fetishes, right?" My chest aches painfully as I force myself to continue. "I'm sure there's some kind of ugly girl fetish, so I haven't given up hope just yet." I roll my eyes self-deprecatingly before turning to Evie. "Oh God, do you remember that guy you went out with and you busted him stealing your panties?" I laugh lightly, my words drawing Evie's angry gaze from Tash to myself, my eyes beseeching her to save me from this painful attention.

She nods slightly, plastering on a huge grin, and

proceeds to tell the story of the panty-stealer, embellishing somewhat and playing to her audience like a master.

Fifteen minutes later, everyone is completely enthralled, allowing me to make a quiet exit. Gathering my trash, I turn to Ethan only to find his eyes glued to me, obviously warring with himself. I know him well enough to know that he desperately wants to defend my honor, but he also wants to respect my, equally desperate, need to let it drop.

"I need to grab a textbook before my next class, I'll see you later." I stand, but before I can move away, his hand gently grips my forearm, preventing my departure. I ignore the heat that follows his touch, my breath stilling as I wait.

"Are you okay?"

I release my breath and force a smile, prepared to play the role I play so well.

"I'm fine, Millhouse." I scrunch my nose humorously, infusing my tone with as much light-heartedness as I can. "Don't even worry about it. She doesn't mean anything, it's just the way she is." I shrug helplessly. "It's just Tash."

Ethan's expression is decidedly pissy so I act fast before he can draw any unwanted attention back to me.

"I'll catch you later." Before he can respond, my feet are propelling me toward the exit, and I pray I make it to my room before the burn behind my eyes inevitably develops into the tears I need to hide.

§

I stand in front of the mirror, the same mirror that held the reflection Evie was gushing over just days ago, and watch the tears silently streaming down my cheeks with morbid curiosity. I feel the familiar tightening in my chest. The ache in my jaw as it clenches tight. As I stare at the reflection I loathe. The image I would give anything to change.

I understand what I look like, I realize there's no changing it, and I do my best to be at peace with it. But hearing Tash actually put a voice to my inner demons has hit me viscerally. Like a punch to the gut that I can't catch my breath from, and the self-hate pulsing through me is painful in its intensity.

I look myself up and down, slowly heatreng the flaws I'm all too familiar with. From the huge mouth that's slightly too big for my face to the hips that will always be a little too big, too wide, no matter how much weight I lose, to the short legs that verge on stumpy. My inner voice is cruelly whispering in my ear, reminding me how disgusting I am, when the sobs finally come, loudly wracking my body. The habitual despair has me once again questioning if I will ever feel like I'm enough. In a world so obsessed with beauty, it is soul destroying when you realize you're so far from that ideal, it's laughable.

Loud thumping on my door distracts me from my pity party and I do my best to calm myself and stop the last little whimpers tormenting me.

"Layla, let me in."

I flinch at the sound of Ethan's voice. How many times does he have to see me like this? Decimated over people's cruelty toward me. It's no wonder he could never see me as more than a friend, I'm lucky he sees me as anything more than some pathetic victim.

"I can hear you, Bug. Let me in."

I grab a tissue, scrubbing it across my face and wiping away the trails of tears, before quickly blowing my nose.

My movement toward the door is stilted. I feel lethargic from the emotional intensity of my break-down and the beginning of a headache is pulsing along my forehead.

Taking a moment to center myself before I open the door, I take a cleansing breath and turn the knob.

Ethan steps into my room wordlessly, wrapping me up in a tight hug, his arms holding me close, his breath tickling my neck.

I allow myself a moment to languish in his comfort, then push away and flash him a smile.

"I'm fine," I promise.

He shakes his head angrily. "She's a bitch, Bug. A complete bitch. Who says something like that? To anyone, let alone a friend!"

My teeth find my bottom lip, and I chew delicately on it, moving across the room and taking a seat on the desk Evie and I share.

"She's not a bitch, she just has no self-awareness. I really think she has no idea how she comes off to other people. She's superficial, but she's not cruel."

He looks at me incredulously. "How can you fucking defend her?"

"Because I refuse to believe that someone who has been my friend for three years would purposely want to hurt me. She has no reason." The flush of embarrassment hits me all over again at the memory of her words. "Really, her only fault is being too honest and saying what everyone else is too considerate to say."

He crosses the room, his stride determined and his expression intense, stopping when he's right in front of me.

"You know why girls give you shit? It's not because you're ugly or because you're fat. That's just the lie they tell themselves." I watch his face closely, entranced by his sincerity, and notice his pulse point in his neck, racing. I sense how hard he is struggling to control his temper.

He steps into me and lifts his hands so they gently cradle the back of my head. He leans down, his forehead against mine, his mouth so close to my own, we're breathing each other's air.

"You are effortless perfection, and they try to crush you, so no one will notice how fucking short they fall in comparison."

His voice is nothing more than a whisper, his words impassioned, and the only thought running through my head?

Please kiss me.

CHAPTER TWELVE

ETHAN

I want to kiss her.

I want to kiss her so fucking bad.

My hand is itching to thread through her hair and roughly pull, exposing her throat to me. I imagine leaning down and running my tongue along the curve of her neck, and I can almost hear her whimpers as my hands skim along her curves.

The air is heavy with anticipation and she's looking at me like I hung the motherfucking moon. Eyes so trusting, and plump lips parted, just begging for me to take a taste. Shallow breaths cause her chest to rise and fall quickly, and I use every ounce of willpower to keep my eyes from straying to her perky tits. The same tits I've wanted to get my hands on since I saw her in a bathing suit, the summer of eighth grade.

"Layla, are you alright, babe?" The door to the room is flung open and Evie comes rushing in. I step back in surprise, distancing myself from Layla, and for a second I swear I see a flash of disappointment in her eyes.

With a single blink, the moment is gone, and I know I must have imagined it.

Suddenly feeling claustrophobic and desperate to get out of this too-small room, I give her a small smile. "I'll leave you guys to talk." I back away before pausing and reaching over to take her hand, squeezing it in a way I hope comforts. "I'll message you later, to make sure you're okay."

She sighs softly, but her fingers flex under my own, offering me her own reassurance. "I'm fine, I promise."

I scowl at her good-humoredly and reiterate. "I'll talk to you later."

Turning, I make my way out of the room, throwing a casual goodbye to Evie, who is watching us with a look of amusement on her face.

Fuck, I need a drink.

Since it's two in the afternoon, I skip the drink and decide to settle for an OJ instead. As I make my way toward the campus juice bar, I feel on edge.

After three years away from Layla, I had forgotten the effect her body has on me. I had also forgotten how frustrating it is to live with a constant case of blue balls and mentally start preparing myself for all the cold showers in my future.

My mind can't stop replaying what just happened between Layla and me, and every step that takes me farther away from her has me questioning what she would have done if I had taken what I wanted.

The walk to the juice bar takes longer than it should, as I'm stopped by a continual stream of people who stop me to say hi. Except they don't really want to say hi to me. They want to say hi to Jackson Miller's son.

My jaw clenches tight after I'm stopped for the fourth time. Usually, I'm able to shrug this stuff off, I've been putting up with it my entire life and to be fair, I get it. My old man is a legend and I understand people wanting to get a piece of him. But when you're the piece they're trying to take, it gets old real quick.

Making a last-minute decision to skip the juice, I make an abrupt turn in the opposite direction and head for my truck. Pulling a cap out of my backpack, I slip it on my head and pull it down low over my eyes, hopeful it'll give off a leave-me-the-fuck-alone vibe.

It seems to do the trick, and I heave a sigh of relief when I make it to the parking lot. I'm climbing into the cab when my phone goes off and I immediately snatch it from my back pocket, hoping it might be Layla. Yeah, can you say pussy?

Dad: You ready for the game on Saturday?

I can't help but laugh at the timing of his message. Despite everything, I love having his unconditional support. I only wish that I shared his love of the game.

That I didn't feel as though I was letting him down every time he was more excited about an exceptional block I made than I was. Every time he celebrated a win harder than I did.

I wish this was a passion we could share, but football had never set my soul on fire the way it did his.

Me: Yeah, good to go. You guys all still coming?

Dad: Of course. Emme wants you to know that she's excited to eat hot dogs and drink soda.

Dad: Also, to see you play, but mostly the hot dogs and soda.

Me: Lol. Little smartass. Tell her I heard a rumor that the school has run out of both.

Dad: No way in hell, she'll torment me for the next two days. Are you free to stop by the house on Sunday?

Me: Sure, what for? Please don't tell me Mom is pregnant again.

. . .

Dad: Now who's the smartass? No, Sports Illustrated is doing a story on past players and I was hoping you could join us for the interview? No pressure, though.

I groan loudly, the sound reverberating around the cab of the truck. It had been a long time since I'd had to do the smile-for-the-camera, Jackson-Miller's-proud-heir schtick. One of the unexpected bonuses of moving to Washington had been the ability to go under the radar a lot more, and I honestly had no idea how much I had craved it.

Scrubbing a hand across my face, I consider if I should do it. Which is stupid as fuck, because I already know I *will* do it. I owe my father that much.

Me: No problem. Ten-ish okay?

Dad: Perfect. We'll see you after the game.

I shove the phone back in my pocket and start the ignition, determined to ignore the interview until Sunday.

Ten minutes later, I pull up to the apartment complex and sit with the engine idling, taking a moment before I head inside. As much as it pains me to admit it, I was lucky to find this place. There was no way I was moving back home after three years away, and going back to a dorm really didn't appeal to me. I have no clue how Layla does it.

Fuck. Layla.

I underestimated how hard being around her again would be. I'd forgotten how just the sway of her ass, or the innocent way she bites her bottom lip when she's deep in thought, makes my dick swell. I'll definitely need to work on the old subtle junk-rearrangement move.

Shaking my head, I quickly shut the engine off, grab my stuff and head upstairs; a hot shower calling my name.

Reaching the apartment, I push through the door, only to hear a loud oomph as the door makes contact with a body on the other side.

Peering through the doorway, I bite back a laugh when I see Seth laid out on his ass, a stunned expression on his face.

"Jesus, Miller, Hulk strength, much?"

"Get up, douchebag." I step over him and head toward the kitchen, looking for a snack.

"Hey, how was Layla when you went to check on her?" Seth follows behind me. "That was some brutal shit, right there. That Tash chick is kind of a bitch."

I pull open the fridge and start pulling out the makings of a sandwich. "Yeah, she's a nasty piece of shit. She was bitching about Lay to me, right before we ran into her and I had to shut it down." I slap the bread together and take a bite, before continuing. "Layla says she's fine, but she always says she's fine." I shrug. "Doesn't mean she is."

Seth nods in agreement. "Well, tell her we've got her back. Mia was ready to bitchslap Tash when she saw Layla rush off. I had to bribe her with chocolate and sex to get her to calm her ass down."

I huff out a laugh. "I'm sure Layla will appreciate your sacrifice, dude."

"She better." He smirks at me. "I'll catch you later. You got the message about the team meeting after training tonight?"

"Yeah, I got it. I'll catch you in the weight room at four." I push off away from the counter and head down the hallway to my room, throwing Seth a goodbye over my shoulder.

I dump my bag on my desk and am about to make my way to the bathroom when my phone goes off again.

Pulling it out, I'm practically fucking giddy when I see Layla's name on the screen.

Layla: Thanks for checking on me today.

Me: I'll always make sure you're okay, Bug.

Layla: Do you remember this?

. . .

I open the attachment she sends and look at the photo. It's a photo-booth picture of us, taken not long after her eighteenth birthday, just before graduation.

I had made the decision to go to college out-of-state and she was pissed at me. Not that she would admit it. Instead, she ignored her own feelings and went out of her way to spend every minute she could with me. It was the perfect storm of pleasure and pain. Heaven and hell wrapped up in one tiny blonde.

Me: Of course, I do. We spent the day at the beach, I scared you with a crab – seriously, when did you become such a girl? – and we spent the night at that traveling fair.

Layla: Omg, I had forgotten about that crab! You were such a jerk! But that was a good day, wasn't it?

Me: It was the best.

It *was* the best. It was also the day I nearly told her how I felt. That night, standing on her porch, she wrapped me in a hug that was so tight I had to use every ounce of restraint to keep my body under control. But she was pressed right up against me, her body completely flush with mine. My face was resting against her neck, and all I could smell was the coconut body wash she was obsessed with. I felt like she was overwhelming every one of my senses, and my dick took notice.

I still remember the look on her face when she realized. Slightly incredulous, and a beautiful pink flush rose up her chest, her neck and finally tinted her cheeks.

She looked so fucking beautiful and I was just about to give in to every instinct I had and take her mouth in the kiss I had been waiting for, for as long as I could remember.

Instead, she stuttered out an embarrassed goodbye and rushed inside, leaving me standing alone, feeling like a total asshole.

I can't help wondering why she's reminding me of that moment. A moment that we never discussed.

My phone sounds, drawing me out of my memories.

Layla: I was always lucky to have you. I don't think I ever told you that, but it's important you know that I always knew it.

A grin slides across my face. She has no idea what she's just done. The hope she's just given me. I won't give up on her. She's meant to be mine and the first opportunity I get, I will make it happen.

CHAPTER THIRTEEN

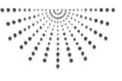

LAYLA

"You want another drink?"

"Uh, yeah, sure." Michael's voice distracts me from the story Seth is telling. "Thanks."

"Same again?"

I consider his question with more thought than you would expect after four beers. I'm not much of a drinker, so they've gone straight to my head and I'm feeling deliciously happy. Probably a little *too* happy.

"I think I'll switch to water." I flash him a quick smile and turn my attention back to Seth. The noise vibrating through *Hound Dog* is making it difficult to hear. Which is saying a lot when you consider just how loud Seth is.

Feeling a gentle tug on my hand, I look back at Michael who is gazing at me with a teasing gleam in his eye. "You sure? One more won't hurt."

I study him carefully through slightly glassy eyes. We've been seeing each other for nearly a month now, and it hasn't been at all what I thought it would be like. The flashy, cocky persona he presents to the world is a far cry from the kind and considerate guy I've gotten to know. I know I can trust him.

"Okay, why not—"

"I'll take a water too, thanks, Michael," Evie interrupts with a grin.

He looks between us as though deciding what to do. I glance at Evie and I don't know why, but I'm grateful for her request.

"Actually, yeah, I will take a water." A flicker of what could be annoyance flashes across Michael's face, but considering my level of happy, it's hard for me to be sure. When a bright smile lights up his face, I'm reassured that I imagined it.

"Whatever the ladies want. I'll be right back."

Watching him walk away, the familiar sense of relief washes over me and I hate myself a little more every time it does.

"Miiiiiilller! You made it, man!" Seth rises from his seat, somewhat wobbly on his feet, and holds out his hand, attempting to do some complicated manly handshake. He fails miserably and falls back on his butt while Ethan stands laughing at him.

Sliding into the booth next to me, he plants a kiss on my cheek. "Hey, Bug." I feel a heated blush spread across my cheeks as I greet him, and he starts up a conversation with the guy across from him.

Things have gotten both better and worse with us over the last month. We've fallen into all our old habits, messaging constantly, sharing meals together and my day generally ends with the two of us on my bed, binge-watching Netflix.

So, yeah, I'm basically in high school again. Which also means my heart pounds anytime he's near me, my skin resembles a tomato anytime he touches me and the worst thing of all? When I'm lying in bed at night and I should be thinking about the guy I'm actually dating? I'm thinking about my best friend. And I want to boob punch myself for being so stupid.

I can't deny that something has changed since the 'Tash incident.' I know it's ridiculous and it couldn't possibly be true, but for a second I honestly believed he was going to kiss me. That moment and his heated expression has tormented me every day since.

I still have no clue what made me send him that message that night. I think I just wanted to remind him that once, no matter how briefly, his body had recognized that I was more than just *Bug*. For one moment I was more than just the girl he had chased dragonflies with or the girl who had suffered through endless hours of *The Simpsons* with him.

"Douchebag, move." I look up to see Michael glaring at Ethan, and my heart drops when I realize how inappropriate this must look. Ethan beside me, his arm casually slung over the seat behind me, and me leaning back into his touch, feeling more relaxed than I have all night.

I expect Ethan to refuse and I'm already anticipating the embarrassment of feeling everyone's eyes on me. Instead, his hand slips down, sliding along my shoulder before giving a gentle squeeze and I have to fight every instinct not to sink into his caress. Wordlessly, he slides along the seat, moving to sit beside the guy he was just talking to – I really should try to learn these guys' names – and gives me a small wink across the table. I can't help my answering smile, although I try to hide it with a small cough.

"Here you go." Michael places our drinks in front of us and after we thank him, Evie nudges me.

"I'm ready to head home, how about you?" I squash down the desire to kiss her. My need to run from this awkwardness is overwhelming and I'm so lucky to have a friend who knows me well enough to not only recognize it, but who also wants to save me from it.

"I am feeling kind of tired." My eyes make contact with Michael's and there's no hiding the frustration this time. He's been a complete gentleman these last few weeks, but I'd have to be an idiot not to have noticed the more frequent touches or the self-deprecating jokes about getting turned down. We've indulged in a few heated make-out sessions, but I've never let it go any further. My heart is just too confused at the moment, and I can't cross that line just yet.

"Okay, I'll see you tomorrow?" I groan inwardly when I remember I had agreed to go on a run with him tomorrow afternoon. I'm beginning to realize that this isn't going to happen with Michael. That until I can get my head sorted about Ethan, it's just cruel to lead someone else on.

"Yeah, sounds good. I'll text you." He nods and begins to move so Evie and I can climb out of the booth. I look up to see Ethan watching me through narrowed eyes and when my feet land on the ground and I take a step away from the table, he takes hold of my hand, pulling it to his mouth and places a soft kiss on my fingertips. I feel that simple touch resonate in the apex of my thighs and suppress the shiver that desperately tries to burst free.

"Bye, Bug."

We throw the group a goodbye and when I turn to leave, Michael pulls me into his arms and brushes his lips across mine. Before he has a chance to deepen the kiss, Evie is dragging me away, urging me on to meet the waiting Uber.

Walking away, it's the sensation of the chaste kiss placed on my fingertips that lingers, and I realize how screwed I am.

Twenty-five minutes later we're curled on her bed binging on chocolate and candy, watching the latest episode of *Riverdale*.

"Jughead's hot." I sigh. "I mean, I know Archie is the obvious choice, but there's something about Jughead that makes me tingle."

"Nope, I'm Archie all the way." She snags a red vine between her teeth and bites down savagely. "Talking about choosing between two guys, what are you going to do about Michael?"

My shoulders sag. "I think I'm going to end it. It just doesn't feel right. I think until I figure out how to get over Ethan completely, I'm kind of a b-i-t-c-h if I keep seeing Michael."

She rolls her eyes at me, groaning. "Bitch, Lay, the word is bitch."

I shove her and steal the bag of Swedish Fish she's hogging. "Whatever. I just don't want to be one."

"Well, I'm Team Ethan all the way. Team Layhan!" She giggles. "And I totally think he wants you."

"Yeah, that's so farfetched, I'm not even going there. Can I admit something?"

"Of course you can." She sits up a little straighter as my tone registers.

"It bothers me how easily we've fallen back into old patterns." My body deflates slightly as I admit this. "I feel weak, like I've given in and by doing that I've given up. He broke my heart and I feel like I'm just handing it back to him saying 'here you go, have at it, break it again,' because it feels inevitable that's what's going to happen."

Evie eyes me thoughtfully. "You're not weak, and anyone who thinks you are has never loved anyone. You can't just get over it because that's the sensible thing to do. That bastard emotion claws its way into your very soul, sinks its fangs in and infects you like a fucking disease." Her voice is tinged with regret, so I reach for her hand, squeezing gently in an effort to comfort, and her expression softens.

"Love isn't so easily shaken off, no matter how much you wish differently. Be kind to your heart, Layla, it's been through enough."

"I'm glad you suggested this." Michael takes a seat at the picnic bench and opens his juice bottle. "I wasn't feeling up to a run after training this morning."

"Are you guys ready for the game tomorrow?" My voice is nervous and high pitched, and I'm praying he doesn't pick up on my trepidation.

Luckily, he seizes on my question and launches into a tirade about how hopeless the Wolves are.

"Seriously, there's no way we can lose to them, they're a joke." My brows arch at the venom in his voice. "You're coming to the game, right?"

I nod my head in confirmation. "Good, I was thinking we could have a celebration dinner after? Chris has said we could borrow his place for the night."

There's no way to miss his implication and he's given me the perfect opening to say what I need to say.

I take a deep breath and swallow down the apprehension that is coursing through me.

"Um, that would be really nice, but I've been thinking, um..." My voice is too hesitant, and I wish I could just say it. "I think maybe, I mean I've had so much fun with you, you're such a great guy, and like, I'm so glad we went out, but..." My voice trails off helplessly and I know I am completely messing this up. Determined to make this as painless as possible, for both of us, I open my mouth to continue when I'm cut off.

"Are you fucking kidding me?" I finally make eye contact with Michael, only to find him glaring at me like I'm a piece of gum stuck to his shoe.

"I've dragged your fat ass around for the last month, I've risked my reputation on a girl who looks like *you*, so fucking ugly, and you're breaking up with *me*?" He laughs cruelly, and my entire body sinks into the warm embrace of numbness as he spews his harsh words at me.

"Un-fucking-believable. Do you really think a guy like me would ever want a girl like you? You're a fucking *joke*, Layla. I was just trying to piss Miller off, and do you know how fucking stupid you are for believing me when I said that wasn't true. How *pathetic* you are for believing that?"

I feel the warmth of tears slide down my cheeks as I listen to his callous words and I wonder what I was thinking, because he's right. How could I have believed it?

"Fucking hell, tell Tash to give me a call. Now that's an ass I'd actually like to tap." With those last words of vitriol thrown at me, he gathers his stuff and walks off without looking back.

I don't know how long I sit here. I have no idea when the tears stop. And I don't realize how cold I am until a warm hand grips my arm and shakes me.

"Layla?" His voice is too soft, and it's overwhelmed by the voice in my head screaming Michael's taunts back to me.

"Layla." The voice, firmer this time, drags me out of my bubble of numbness. I'm wrapped up in two huge arms and a familiar woodsy scent tickles my nose.

Slowly, I lift my arms and return the embrace, desperate to be comforted in any way I can.

"You with me, Bug?" He pulls back, and I find myself staring into Ethan's hazel eyes, admiring the golden ring that always made them so beautiful to look at. I nod slightly, the only response I have in me.

"Okay, we're gonna go back to your dorm and then you're going to tell me exactly what happened. Can you walk?" I get to my feet and allow him to wrap an arm around me as we make the short walk back to my room.

My mind is a frenzied mess right now, but the one thought screaming the loudest? How lucky I am that Ethan has always got me.

§.

"The guy's an asshole."

I have to give Ethan credit. His tone holds no recriminations. No sense of I-told-you-so. Just genuine anger.

"It is what it is." I shrug in an effort to appear unconcerned, taking a sip of the mug of hot chocolate Ethan made for me. But the fact is, all I can hear are the words Michael threw at me so heartlessly.

Fat. Ugly. Pathetic. Joke.

Words I heard on repeat through my childhood. Words that my inner-witch whispers to me when my mind gets too quiet.

Ethan busies himself searching under my bed for my secret stash of candy.

"There's nothing there."

He glances up at me in surprise. "What?"

"There's no secret stash. I don't do that anymore. If

you want candy, I think there's some in the cupboard next to the desk."

He follows my finger and walks to the cupboard, pulling out a pack of cookies that he tears into before taking a seat on my bed and placing them in between us.

"You know, he's probably sitting at home right now, crying in his Cheerios that you dumped his ass."

My answering snort is self-deprecating. "I think we both know that's not true." My fingers tighten around the mug, knuckles turning white, and my eyes flit around the room nervously before I continue. "I'm not the kind of girl that guys waste time regretting."

Ethan jumps up and begins pacing around the small room.

"That's total bullshit and you know it."

The condescending tone in his voice irks me, and I feel myself fire up.

"What I know, *Ethan*, is guys like Michael don't end up with girls like me."

"Guys like Bradshaw? Assholes, you mean? You're right, they don't get girls like you, you're too fucking good for them."

His voice rises angrily, imploring me to hear him. Instead, his easy dismissal of the truth only infuriates me.

"Guys like Michael." I lean forward, my body vibrating with rage. "Guys like you! Men who can have anyone they want. They don't fall in love with the plain girl, Ethan. To say differently is a bold-faced lie."

His head snaps back as if I've slapped him and he

wears an expression of shock. I watch closely as he struggles for words while I fight to regain my composure before I admit too much.

"You know I love you, Bug." The sincerity in his voice is my undoing and after all these years, I break.

"Not in the way I needed you to." My voice cracks and I loathe how desperate I sound. I slump back against the wall in defeat. "You never saw me the way I wanted you to."

Silence descends on the room, suffocating me, and for the first time in my life, the desire to be away from him overpowers the need to be near him.

I scramble off the bed, dumping my mug on the desk and heading for the door when his voice stops me in my tracks.

"I saw you, Layla." His eyes are feral as he thumps his chest. "*I* fucking saw you, every single day."

CHAPTER FOURTEEN

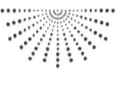

ETHAN

I listen to the bullshit she's spewing at me and I can feel the rage pulsating through me. All these years she's thought I was out of her league when I spent my entire life chasing her around like a lost fucking puppy?

Adrenaline is pumping through my veins and I feel out of control, like my brain can't process what's happening right now. I continue to pace the room like a caged animal, which is ironic since that is exactly what I feel like.

Layla pushes up off the bed and I watch her move toward the door, her eyes glassy with unshed tears, and I finally lose control.

"I saw you, Layla. *I* fucking saw you, every single day."

She pauses, but just for a moment, before continuing her path to the door. Her head shakes back and forth as though trying to convince herself my words aren't true.

"You need to leave." Her words stop me in my tracks, stunning me into a stillness I didn't think I was capable of right now.

She stands in the open doorway, her hand on the knob. I hold her stare, and we continue in this stand-off until tears begin to silently fall down her cheeks.

"Go," she chokes out. "Please."

Fuck. That.

I stride forward aggressively, and I don't miss the way her eyes widen as she realizes my intent.

Reaching her, I use my right hand to push the door shut and thread my left through her hair. Using my hips, I slam her back against the now-closed door and pin her body to it. My need for her makes it impossible to be gentle. There will be plenty of time for that later.

I lean down and run my nose along the length of her neck, her sweet scent overwhelms me, and I breathe in deeply, wanting nothing more than to be overwhelmed by this woman.

The way her body responds to mine, the shallow breaths, and the almost involuntary shiver, gives me the confidence to continue. My teeth find purchase on that sweet spot where her neck meets her shoulder and I bite down, roughly, desperate to mark her. Her answering groan has both my dick and my resolve, hardening.

I tighten my grip on her hair and my other hand snakes up to loosely grip her throat and I squeeze gently. Her eyes fly up to meet mine, and the excitement I see in them has me pushing my body deeper into hers.

Unable to hold back, I press my mouth against hers and slide my tongue along her lips. My restraint shatters as her sweet taste hits my tongue and a feral groan rumbles out from deep within my throat.

Her hands are clawing at my shoulders, trying to pull me closer and I suck her bottom lip between my own as my hands tangle in her hair. Every breathless whimper she makes has my cock jumping against my zipper, desperate for freedom, and when my tongue finally enters her mouth, she writhes against me, uncontrollably.

Years of pent-up hunger has me taking her mouth aggressively, and Layla responds with an intensity that matches my own.

"You taste so fucking good." My voice is raspy and sounds foreign to my own ears.

"Oh God, don't stop."

Our kiss is savage, with a ferocity I didn't expect, a wildness that is welcomed. I grab her ass and lift, her legs immediately wrap around my waist and her elbows land on my shoulders, her hands grabbing my hair and pulling, as though she can't control herself.

My lips tilt up in a smirk against her mouth and I move us across the room to sit on her bed. Her mouth doesn't leave my skin the entire time. Kissing, licking, and biting her way along my jaw until she reaches the spot under my ear that has my eyes rolling back and my chest vibrating with need.

I reconnect our mouths, licking along the seam and she opens with a groan. I ensnare her tongue between my lips and suck, reveling in the way Layla wiggles against me.

"*Fuck*." I release the word with a hiss when her jean-covered pussy rolls over my cock. She pulls back and looks at me with a wicked glint in her eye and I fucking love that she can still shock me.

My hands reach down and pull up her plain white tee, revealing her tits, all plump and just begging for my mouth on them.

"Ethan?" Her voice, sounding pained, jolts me out of the fog I had fallen into. I search her eyes, terrified that she's going to tell me to stop.

Instead, she leans into my touch, rests her forehead against mine and rasps out, "Touch me."

My. Fucking. Pleasure.

I bend forward and place my mouth on the swell of her breast, sweeping my tongue out to taste her skin, loving the way goosebumps follow the path of my tongue. My right hand toys with her other tit, squeezing it and rolling the nipple through her bra, eliciting the kinds of filthy moans I've fantasized about falling from her mouth.

"That feels so good, keep doing that, 'kay?" A ridiculous sense of pride hits me at the mindlessness in her voice, so unlike Layla. And I fucking did that.

"I'm not gonna stop, baby, I've needed this for so long." My voice is muffled by her neck and my hands are going crazy, trying to touch every part of her. Every part that has been off limits to me, needs to be marked.

I involuntarily thrust up when her teeth graze along

my jaw and I squeeze my eyes shut in an effort to control myself. Because I'm seconds away from blowing in my pants right now, and that's really not how I want this to end.

"Shit, I love you, Lay," I breathe out. "I love you, so fucking much."

Her body stills completely, and when I look up, she's staring at me wide-eyed. I'm not sure if it's happiness or horror I can see, and I suddenly feel the cold wash of nerves hit me.

"What?" Her voice is small and timid. The voice she reserves for people she's unsure of. A voice she has never used with me.

"What?" I throw her question back at her because fuck if I'm going to pretend I didn't say it or act like I haven't wanted this to happen since I was twelve years old. This girl is it for me, and if there's any chance she feels the same way, I refuse to let her run away.

"What did you say?"

"I said I love you." My voice is firm, controlled.

"Well, you shouldn't!" Her voice is neither of those things. She jumps off my lap, pulling her shirt down as she does, and I guess it's her turn to pace the room.

"Telling someone you love them when you're dry-humping them is a lot different than telling a friend you love them. Why would you do that?"

I try to hide my amusement when her voice reaches dog-whistle levels.

"I understand that." She throws her hands up in the air and I'm not sure if she's more frustrated with my answer, or my calmness.

"What?" she shrieks.

Standing up, I move toward her calmly, arms slightly aloft, for what reason I have no fucking idea. Maybe, in surrender?

"Come and sit down, Bug, we should talk." I take hold of her arm and gently guide her back to her bed. She comes, but she shakes her head the entire way.

"You can't call me Bug anymore."

I bite back a laugh. "Why is that?"

"Because, because," she sputters, and I have to admit I'm loving this slightly neurotic Layla. She's fucking funny.

"Because nothing. I'm still gonna call you Bug, nothing's changed." I shrug nonchalantly. I do it simply to piss her off and see what happens, and when her eyes practically pop out of her head, I have no regrets.

"Everything has changed. *Everything.*"

"Nothing has changed." I kneel in front of her so we're eye level, and cup her head in my hands. "From what I can gather from that bullshit you were giving me before, you have feelings for me. Right?" I raise an eyebrow, challenging her.

A beautiful blush spreads across her cheeks.

"I'll take that as a yes." I lean in and brush my lips across her mouth and the small sigh she exhales in response has me wanting to deepen the kiss. Instead, I break away, and sit back on my heels, needing some distance between us if I'm going to continue.

"I've been in love with you for as long as I can remember, Lay." She shakes her head again, in denial. "Yes. And now that I know how fucking stupid we've both been." Her eyes narrow indignantly. "Don't look at me like that. I'm kind of judging you for being completely clueless to how I felt. It's not like I was fucking subtle."

She pushes me away and I fall on my ass.

"That is such crap! You never gave me any clue that you liked me, Ethan Miller. Don't you dare try and rewrite our history." Her lips are pursed and her jaw clenched as she glares down at me. I laugh loudly at her fierceness. Neurotic Layla was fun, but it's good to have the real one back.

"Don't laugh at me, *Millhouse*," she scoffs.

This time my hands are definitely held up in surrender.

"Okay, okay, it's *possible* I wasn't as obvious as I thought I was, but I was way more obvious than you." She starts to interrupt me, but I plow on, determined to have my say. "None of that matters, anyway. I was stupid, you were stupid." Again her mouth opens to cut me off. "But– *but*—" I hold a finger up to silence her. "Let's just stop being stupid, okay?"

She snaps her mouth shut and stares at me silently for a beat. Then another. For one painfully long moment, I worry that she won't take this leap with me.

She climbs down off the bed and sits on the floor beside me. Taking my hand in hers, she threads her fingers through mine and stares at them, almost wondrously.

"Will you go on a date with me?" She doesn't look at me but remains fixated on our hands.

"Yes." This gets her attention, and I get eye contact.

Her expression is a mix of fear and hope and I hate that I haven't been able to erase all her apprehension. But I will, there's not a doubt in my mind about that.

"Now?" she pushes.

"Fuck, yes, let's go." I stand up, dragging her with me and head straight to the door.

"Wait, *wait*." She laughs. "Give me a second."

I blatantly watch her as she straightens her clothes and runs a brush through her hair, my eyes devouring every inch of her. I have no idea how we ended up here today, but I'm thankful we did, and I'll do whatever I have to, to make sure I don't fuck it up.

"Ready." She takes my hand and we begin to walk to the door, but I stop her as she reaches for the handle and press her against the wall.

"We'll figure this out. I promise I won't ruin us, Bug."

She smiles softly before standing on her tiptoes and pressing her mouth to mine.

"Haven't you figured it out yet, Ethan?" Her tongue sneaks out and steals a taste of my lips. "I've been waiting for you to ruin me for the longest time."

CHAPTER FIFTEEN

LAYLA

*H*ow did this happen? How did this day go from a nightmare to a dream?

I'm still trying to process everything that has happened over the last half hour. The words, the touching, the kissing, oh good Lord the *kissing*. He exceeded every single fantasy I've ever had about him. And trust me, I've had a lot of them.

Although, there will be consequences for the stupid comments.

I'm currently being pulled toward the parking lot, and when I glance at Ethan, he has the biggest, goofiest smile on his face. I still can't quite believe I'm the one that put it there.

"Quit staring at me, Lay." His voice rouses me from my not-so-subtle admiration.

"Ugh, get over yourself, I was looking at that guy behind you, he's hot." Ethan's face contorts and his eyes cloud over. He whips his head around and scowls at the poor guy behind him. This is *so* weird.

Releasing my hand, he slides his arm around my shoulder and pulls me in tight. This is something he has done a thousand times over the years, but there's something so different about this touch. Like he's claiming me, which is ludicrous, and something I really shouldn't like the idea of so much.

"How about *Delilah's*?"

My mouth immediately starts to water at the idea of one of their burgers. *Delilah's* is a low-key diner tucked away in a scummy-looking alley, only a few blocks away from campus. It might not look like much, but the food is to die for.

"Oh, God, yes please," I groan.

Ethan stops in his tracks, looking down at me with an expression I can't quite identify.

"Say that again."

I roll my eyes, laughing at his demand. "C'mon, you should know by now the way to a chubby girl's heart is through her stomach. Feed me."

I start walking but am held back when the arm around my shoulders stays attached to the very non-moving, very annoyed-looking guy beside me.

"Don't do that."

My heart sinks a little when I realize what I said. "It was just a joke, Ethan, relax. Let's go." I try to pull him forward, but he stands resolute.

"It wasn't a joke and we both know it. I've never let you pull that shit with me before, I don't know why you think I'm going to start now."

He's right, he never has, always calling me out any time I use self-deprecation as a shield. Which, honestly, annoys the hell out of me. It's my best defense mechanism, and when I'm stripped of it, I'm left feeling way too vulnerable.

Just like now.

"*Fine.*"

He smirks down at me while I glower right back at him. Seriously, sometimes people that know you too well are a pain in the butt.

"Good, let's go, then."

We change our direction slightly since we can walk to *Delilah's* and make our way there, hand in hand.

Ethan chats away throughout the entire walk and it turns out he's pretty touchy-feely with the girls he dates, because he spends an inordinate amount of time with his hands on me. Running his hand up and down my back, playing with my hair and teasing along the back of my neck with his fingertips. Every touch has my body humming in anticipation.

I can't deny that our exchange has rattled me, though, and instead of concentrating on the wonderful strangeness of his intimate caresses, I find myself scanning everyone we pass, looking for the sneers, or laughter I expect at the sight of us together.

It occurs to me that I never felt this way with Michael, but I quickly realize it's because he was never particularly tactile with me, at least not in public. To passers-by, we would have simply looked like friends.

After a ten-minute walk that feels like an eternity, we make our way into the diner. It's relatively quiet, which pleases me, but it's still pretty early. I have no doubt it'll be packed in an hour or two.

"What about that booth over there?" Ethan points to a table over in the corner and I nod, happy that it's slightly out of the way.

We get settled and the waitress comes to take our order before we have a chance to talk. She goes straight to Ethan because let's face it, she's a woman and she has eyes.

"I'll have fried chicken, the loaded cheese fries and a chocolate shake, thanks." He glances across at me. "Bacon cheeseburger, no pickle or tomato, sweet potato fries and a caramel frappe?"

I can't help but laugh softly at his eagerness to impress me. Have I mentioned how weird this is?

I hold my thumb and forefinger up, so they're only heatreng apart. "*So* close," I answer and turn to the waitress. "Peach iced tea instead of the frappe, please."

She nods, noting our orders down before turning to leave, but not before she throws a little wink Ethan's way. I roll my eyes.

The silence that follows feels a bit awkward, as though we've both realized this is supposed to be a date and we don't do that. Date, I mean. Although, I guess we do now. Huh, how about that. *So weird.*

I miss the confidence I felt back in my dorm room. It all seemed so straightforward twenty minutes ago. I also miss his mouth on me, but that's another subject entirely.

"Are you ready for Halloween?" His voice snaps me out of my melancholy thoughts and I shake my head.

"I haven't even thought about it. Evie normally

drags me to Greek Row and we party hop." I grimace. "It's awful."

"Yeah, that doesn't really sound like your thing." He laughs. "She won't mind if I tag along, will she?"

"Uh, no I don't think so." I purse my lips. "She's kind of a fan of yours."

"Ah, she's a smart girl, that one. So, I promised Emme I would take her trick or treating, you want to come with us? I know she'd love to see you."

"Yeah, I'd love to. I actually owe her a bag of gummy worms."

"Why?"

"Last time I was there, I bet her she couldn't rub her tummy and pat her head at the same time." I shake my head in amusement at the memory. "I'm pretty sure she hustled me."

"Wait, when did you see Emme?" he asks in confusion.

"When I was home on break."

"Oh, you ran into her?"

"No." I try to keep the exasperation from my voice. "I went to see her. I visit Emme and your mom and dad whenever I'm home."

I don't know what I've said that's so shocking, but he's staring at me as if he has no idea what to say.

Thankfully, we're interrupted by the arrival of our food. We spend the next forty-five minutes planning our Halloween; trick or treating followed by parties later that night, and I have to admit I'm not sure how to feel about this 'date.'

On the one hand, I'm relieved that our earlier

confessions haven't made things awkward. But, on the other hand, now that we're sitting here, it's feeling remarkably like every other meal we've shared over the years.

I don't know what I expected, but I think it was more than this.

"What's going on in there?" He reaches across the table and tucks a strand of hair behind my ear and gently taps my temple.

"This is weird."

"No, it's not."

"Yeah, but that's *why* it's weird. Don't you think after what happened, things should be a little strange?"

He considers what I've said and continues to stuff his face with cheese fries.

Finally, he points a fry at me and asks, "You know what I think?"

"That's kind of why I asked, Millhouse."

"Have you ever noticed that you only call me Millhouse when you're annoyed? I'm beginning to think it's not the term of endearment I always believed it was. But—" he shoves the fry in his mouth, "—I digress. I don't think our relationship is really going to change."

I open my mouth to point out the bright, shiny, flashing flaw in his argument, but he cuts me off.

"Think about it. I've been in love with you for years." I wiggle in my seat, uncomfortable with how casually he keeps throwing around the 'L' word. "And you've had feelings for me for years, right?" He smiles broadly at my nod. "So, nothing has actually changed for us, we've just stopped being stupid and admitted it."

I raise my eyebrows and glare at him. "You really think nothing is going to change?" I snort incredulously.

"Of course *things* are going to change, Bug. But, *we're* not."

He gets up and moves around the table so that he's sitting beside me.

"Like, whenever you think I'm being completely ridiculous you do this thing with your lips, and I always want to do this." He leans over and loosely cradles my throat with his hand, before biting down on my bottom lip and swiping his tongue along it to soothe the sting.

I instinctively relax into his touch, needing so much more than he can give me in the middle of a bustling diner.

"We're going to be fine," he whispers.

"How can you be so sure?"

And with all the confidence in the world, he responds, "Because I won't let us *not* be."

The music is too loud and there are too many bodies cramped in a too small space, but somehow, I'm actually having fun. Believe me, I'm surprised too.

I giggle as Evie pulls out some wicked dance moves in an attempt to entice me to dance with her.

Ethan pulls me in closer to him, so my back is flush up against his front and leans down to whisper in my ear.

"You should go and dance, baby, I'd definitely like to watch that." His voice, all growly and sexy, tickles my ear and holds a note of hunger.

I stare at him, with his ridiculous Harry Potter-style glasses and lightning bolt scar drawn on his forehead and wonder how I got this lucky. This last week has been amazing and to be honest, I'm still kind of in shock.

There has been a lot of talking, an abundance of confessions and I've spent the week vacillating between complete happiness and overwhelming sadness. Every intimate touch and whispered endearment is counterbalanced by an intense feeling of loss for the years we missed out on. It makes me so damn mad that Ethan was right. We were so very stupid.

But we've made it. We're where we want to be now, and Ethan was, once again, right. Although I'll never admit that to his face. Our relationship really hasn't changed too much. The big difference is the touching. So much touching. Swoony, thigh-clenching, panty-melting touching.

"Where'd you just go?"

Leaning back against him, I sigh softly as his soft voice pulls me from my thoughts. "Somewhere really, really nice."

"Ugh, you two are disgusting." Evie grabs my hand and pulls me away. "Come. I need to pee."

I notice she doesn't give a second look to her date for the night, which disappoints me.

Jonathan is a cute, gamer geek who plays alongside

Ethan, and I was hopeful she might like him. Because, well, double dates and all that.

We make our way to the off-limits downstairs bathroom Ethan told us about, and I'm grateful we're in Ethan's teammates' frat house so we can avoid the lines of people doing who knows what, in the upstairs bathrooms.

I keep my back turned while Evie pees, and we chat idly while I reapply my lip gloss.

"What do you think of Jonathan?"

"Meh, he's okay, I guess."

I bite the inside of my cheek at her answer. "But he's not Tyler?"

I hear the toilet flush and she appears beside me. "Nobody is like Tyler Bailey." Her face softens at the mention of his name, and I send up a silent prayer that she gets her chance with him.

"So, I can tell Ethan to stop with the setups?"

"Oh, hell no. I still need to have a little fun while Tyler figures his shit out, and I am in no way opposed to doing that with hot football players." She dries her hands on the paper towels so thoughtfully left out at the sink. I guess hand towels are too high class for frat boys.

"Oh God, please don't tell him that. He's convinced that he's destined to be some kind of matchmaker extraordinaire. When you agreed to go out with Jonathan tonight, he tried to make me call him Mr. Romance."

We spend a few minutes engaging in some trivial gossip and laughing over our Minions costumes. The fitted yellow t-shirt, black suspenders, and short jean-shorts were the perfect compromise between her desire to be sexy and my need to be comfortable.

Our voices echo through the narrow stairway as we make our way back to the party, but it dies on our lips at the sight that greets us.

Ethan is being held back by three of his teammates, a trickle of blood sliding down his chin and a feral look in his eye.

On the floor, holding his jaw and with a bloody nose, is Michael.

&

"What were you *thinking*?"

It took five guys, Evie, and me to drag him out of the party. Michael was intent on provoking a fight and we left with his vile comments ringing in our ears.

"I was thinking that the guy's a dickhead and he deserved to be pounded." Ethan's voice is petulant, and I know he's annoyed we put an end to the fight before it really began.

"Yes, he is, and yes, he does. But not by you. Let's leave the pounding to karma, 'kay?"

We're in his apartment and he's sitting on the kitchen counter, my discarded suspenders and his Harry Potter glasses beside him, his bare feet swinging. I reach up to dab some ointment on the small cut along his bottom lip, trying to hide my amusement at his pout.

"So, what happened anyway? Why'd you start something with him?" I steel myself for what's to come, knowing Ethan would only behave like that in defense of his family, or me.

His face clouds over, but when his eyes meet mine it clears, and the familiar look of mischief replaces it. He shakes his head and slides down off the counter, looming over me. The air in the room suddenly shifts.

His nose grazes along mine and his mouth is inches from my own.

"Hi," he whispers.

My core pulses at that one word and I have to suppress the urge to push my body into his, seeking the friction I need.

While there has been a lot of touching these past five days, we haven't crossed that line yet.

Five days. I can't believe it's only been five days. I never believed I would be ready to sleep with someone after only five days, to make myself that vulnerable. But there is no one I trust more than Ethan, and with his body so close to mine, his breath mingling with my own, I'm about ready to jump him.

"Hi."

His lips crash against mine and my mouth opens on a sigh. Goosebumps break out across my skin when his tongue finds mine, teasing and tasting.

My hands tangle in his hair, pulling him closer and his hands slide down my body, shamelessly groping until he has a handful of butt and he grinds our pelvises together, causing little zings of electricity to pop in all the good spots.

He lifts my feet off the ground and heads in the

direction of his room, never once breaking the connection our mouths have created.

Slamming the door behind us with his foot, he gently places me down and breaks the kiss. We've made out a lot this week, but something about this feels different. Apparently, I'm not the only one who thinks so.

"Is this okay?" His voice is thick, as though talking is difficult, and I bite my lip as I consider his question. Is this okay? It's *more* than okay.

"Yes."

His hands are back on me in a flash, pulling at my clothes until they find the warmth of my skin and he exhales a ragged breath. I can see him attempting to get himself under control, so I take a step back putting some distance between us.

Slowly, I pull my t-shirt over my head, kick my Converse off my feet and shimmy out of my jean shorts. A shiver travels down my spine, initially from the chill in the air, but when I see the look in his eyes, it turns into a ripple of anticipation.

I stand before him in my pink cotton panties and black lace bra, the one with the small rip along the edge of the lace cup, and his eyes roam all over my body. I feel a twinge of self-consciousness at his blatant perusal.

"I wasn't expecting this to happen. I would have worn something sluttier if I had known." I try to disguise my nervousness with bravado.

Finding his voice, he replies, "Slutty, huh? I'm not

sure you could ever look slutty, Bug. You're too sweet." His eyes alight with kind humor.

I feel an intense pang of doubt overwhelm me. I want Ethan to want me. I want him to crave me the way I crave him, and I'm scared he's right; I'm not sure I could ever be that girl. But I refuse to let insecurity spoil this moment.

"I could be slutty if I wanted to be." My voice is quietly defiant, and his answering smirk riles me. Before I can get too inside my head, he steps forward, crowding me and invading my space.

He leans down, running his nose along my jaw and my knees almost buckle as he overwhelms all my senses.

"You wanna be slutty, Bug?" His lips kiss a path toward my ear. "You want to be my little slut? Just for me?" Teeth bite down on my lobe, sending a jolt straight to my core. "Only for me?"

I can't breathe. His proximity and the filthy things he's saying leave me capable of one word only.

"Please."

CHAPTER SIXTEEN

ETHAN

*G*oddamn. She takes my breath away. Hearing that one word fall from her gorgeous mouth and knowing she's giving me a piece of herself that's just for me, has me rock-hard.

I lose control, and before she can register what is happening, I've removed my jeans and Henley, and I reach for her, intent on making her mine.

Mine. I want to bang on my chest and growl the word like a fucking caveman.

I pull her flush against me and I know the exact moment she feels my hard-on pressed against her stomach because a pink flush heats her face.

I lean down and lick along her collarbone and using my index finger I pull down the cup of her bra exposing her breast and her perfectly pebbled pink nipple. I'm practically salivating at the sight and before she can stop me, my mouth latches on and I suck hard before biting down, eliciting a moan that has my cock standing so tall, the head is peeking out of my boxers.

Reaching around, I unhook her bra and slide the straps down her arms. I pull back, so I have a better view of her in the somewhat darkened room, and my fingertips trace along the curve of her hips.

She's holding on to my shoulders, her nails digging in, and when I glance up, I see that she has her eyes closed.

"Baby, look at us." To my relief, she opens them immediately and all I see in them is need. The need to be loved. The need to be fucked. And I am more than happy to oblige on both counts.

I take hold of her hand and guide it to slide across the softness of her belly, down to her panties. Her breath stutters and that one simple sound urges my fingers lower.

"Shit," I hiss out when our fingers slide along her pussy and I feel how wet she is. "You're so fucking wet, Lay. You want me to do filthy things to this little pussy?"

Her head falls forward against my chest, and her breathing is ragged. When our fingers find her clit, she moans so loudly that I'm grateful Seth and Mia aren't here. Nobody gets to hear my girl like this, except me.

Her knees start to buckle, and she pulls her hand out, grabbing on to my forearm to steady herself and, being the perverted fucker I am, I grin like a fool as she wipes the smell of her pussy all over my skin.

I wrap my arms around her waist, settling my hands over her ass and walk us backward until I feel the edge of my bed behind my knees. Spinning us around, I hold her body close to mine with one arm and lean down until the other finds the mattress and I gently lay her down.

This is the closest we've been to naked with each other and I can't stop my hand from finding its way to my dick and jerking roughly through the cotton of my boxers. She's fucking perfect, all soft curves that feel stupidly incredible against the hardness of my body.

I shake myself out of creeper mode and climb up on the bed, nudging her legs open and crawling between them. My dick is painfully hard as it settles against the warmth of her pussy and I have to squeeze my eyes closed and think about football stats until I get myself under control.

"Ethan?" Her voice is soft and holds a note of humor. "Are you okay?"

"Uh huh," I grit out.

"Are you sure?"

"Stop talking, I really need you to stop talking, right now."

She giggles. Fucking giggles and my cock jumps at the sound. Without thinking, I roll my hips and we groan in unison when I make contact with her clit.

Sucking in a steadying breath, I sit up and kneel between her legs before reaching for her panties. Those sweet-as-fuck pink panties that are so Layla. I pull them down as slowly as I can manage in an effort not to appear like the sex-starved maniac I currently feel.

I throw them over my shoulder, loving the smile it draws from Layla, and find myself staring at the most perfect cunt I have ever seen. Pink and pure, the lips glisten with her juices and my tongue swipes across my lip, desperate for a taste.

"Can I…?" My voice trails off raggedly and I sigh in relief at her answering nod.

Leaning down, I trail a finger along her slit, the wetness making my finger glide easily. I keep my eyes locked on Layla and when she closes her eyes and arches slightly off the bed, I take advantage of her incoherence and slide a finger inside her. It's so fucking tight I feel almost light-headed at the thought of my dick sliding home.

She moans at the sensation, her eyes still shut tight.

"Layla, open your eyes, baby, I want you to watch." She struggles to open them, fighting the pleasure that's forcing them closed, and as soon as I see those dark brown eyes on me, I lie down and put my face right where my dick wants to be. I reach down and give him a hard, quick stroke to calm him down. He'll get his turn.

I trail my lips along her thigh, placing open-mouthed kisses and sucking lightly, while my finger continues to torment her. When I reach the apex of her thighs, I remove my finger and replace it with my tongue, swiping it along her pussy and then sucking her clit between my lips roughly.

"Oh my God." She bolts up off the bed and I reach up with my left hand, pushing her back down and keeping an anchoring palm on her stomach.

Letting go of her clit, I circle it with my tongue and begin alternating between gentle flicks and harsh sucks. I slide two fingers into her this time, and scissor my fingers, stretching her in preparation before I curl them and hit the spot that has her jerking in pleasure.

Her hands slam down on my head, fingers curling in my hair and she shamelessly grinds herself against my face.

"OhmyGodohmyGodohmyGodohmyGod," she chants over and over, and when I lift my eyes to look up at her, I find her staring at me, wide-eyed.

Pulling out my fingers, I replace them with my tongue and start savagely tongue-fucking her while my fingers tease her clit.

She screams out in a very un-Layla-like way, and her pussy clenches around my tongue as she comes. I'm dry-humping the mattress below me uncontrollably, the sounds she's making causing my cock to throb and making me desperate to come.

When her orgasm seems to be fading, I slow the movements of my tongue and fingers but reach up to give her tit a squeeze and pinch her nipple, which causes a helpless whimper to escape her lips.

When she seems a bit more coherent and has loosened her grip on my hair, I sit back and quickly remove my boxer briefs, stroking my dick as I watch her flushed face intently.

It's not long before she's ogling me, her eyes fixated on the flex of my arm and I hide a smirk when she folds her legs up and closes her thighs, rubbing them together in, what I assume is, an attempt to get the friction she needs.

"You need to come again, already, baby?" I ask, breathing harshly.

She keeps her gaze fixed on the movements of my hand and nods her head emphatically. She's so fucking cute.

Opening her thighs, I kneel down and hold her hip with one hand. When the skin underneath goes white, I curse myself and loosen my grip slightly. Lying down so I'm hovering over her, I brush a kiss across her lips. She still tastes like the candy she ate earlier at the party.

"I love you." Her eyes close on a sigh and she smiles softly at me.

Scooting back, I grip my erection and slide it through her slit, coating myself in her cum. I tease the head of my cock around her clit and her strangled groan has my dick leaking, the sensation so intense.

Shit. "I just need to grab a condom."

I turn to move, but she grabs my arm, stopping me.

"Wait, I, uh, I'm on the pill."

Surprise quickly turns to excitement. "I'm clean, Lay, I promise."

She reddens at my words.

"I've never, uh, I'm a..." She stumbles over her words in what I assume is embarrassment, but when her meaning sinks in, I fall forward on top of her, practically crushing her, my hard-on resting on her stomach.

I kiss her ferociously, and it's a mess of tongue and teeth; sloppy and loud, but quite possibly the best kiss of my life.

Reaching between us, I take hold of myself and slide between the lips of her pussy, nudging the head at her entrance. I'm holding myself over her and I break our kiss, needing to watch as I enter her.

She lifts her head slightly and our foreheads meet as we both watch the tip slide in. It slips in easily and when I feel the heat of her clench my head, a fierce growl rumbles from deep in my chest.

Layla has a hand gripped on my shoulder and when I push farther and meet resistance, her nails bite deeply into my skin and her head falls back onto the mattress.

I turn my attention from the porn-worthy view of our connection and place my lips by her ear.

"Relax, baby. I need you to relax, okay?"

She nods, but her eyes are wide with worry. I decide that ripping the Band-Aid off is the way to go and, taking a deep breath I pray I'm right.

Taking her mouth again, I kiss her until I feel her relax under me and then with one deep thrust, I bottom out inside her.

She rips her mouth away from mine and cries out. I take hold of one breast and roll the nipple between my fingers while my mouth falls to the other one, my tongue teasing the puckered tip.

It doesn't take long before I feel her move under me, rolling her hips in an attempt to get some friction. I pull my mouth away from her breasts and look down at her.

"Are you okay?" The idea that I've hurt her badly, kills me.

"You need to move, Ethan, I need you to make me come. Please." Her voice holds a note of urgency I've never heard before.

Pushing myself back up, I pull out of her slowly. She's unlike anything I've ever felt before, all warm, wet and tight. That, combined with the knowledge that this is the girl of my dreams, has my balls tightening and the need to come is overwhelming. I force myself to go slow with shallow thrusts until I'm positive she's acclimated completely.

When her hips start to move up to meet mine, I begin to push in deeper, rotate my hips and mix up my speed. I listen to every breathless sigh, every moan, taking note of what she likes.

"You're so fucking tight and wet. Do you hear that?" I slam into her. "You hear how wet you are for me?"

Her eyes roll back, and she groans loudly. My girl is loud in the bedroom and it turns me the fuck on.

"Harder, please, I need it harder."

I grab her ass and lift it slightly off the bed and pound into her as hard as I can. I need her to come because I can feel the tingle start at the base of my spine and I know I can't hold off my own orgasm much longer.

Removing one of my hands from her ass, I reach between us and start rubbing her clit in fast circles.

"Oh my fucking God, Ethan! I'm coming, I'm coming, please don't stop. *Fuuuuuuuuuck.*"

I feel her pussy clench around me.

"Goddamn it, Layla, you're choking my dick so fucking good. You feel how good that is? How good we are?" My movements become erratic as I feel the orgasm pulse through her. My head falls to her shoulder, and as my own orgasm hits me and I fill her with my cum, I hear her voice whispering, *"oh fuck, oh fuck, so good, it feels so good, oh fuck."*

When we finally come down from our high, I roll us over so that she is on top of me and we lie wrapped up in each other. A chuckle rumbles from my chest and Layla pulls back, glaring at me incredulously.

"Are you *laughing* at me?"

"You swore, Bug." I laugh. "I don't think I've ever heard you swear before. My dick has mad skills."

She punches me in my arm. "Oh my God, you're ridiculous."

I pull her back down to me, my mouth already craving another taste of her.

"That was really nice," she says softly.

"Nice? *Nice?* Now you're just being mean, that was fucking phenomenal."

I feel her smile against my skin. "Okay, it was phenomenal, I'll give you that." She presses her hips into mine and I feel my cock start to thicken at the friction.

"You know what else it was?" Her voice distracts me.

"What?"

She scrunches her nose up. "Messy."

I bark out a laugh. That was not where I was hoping she was going.

"I'll go and grab a washcloth, wait here." I move to stand up when the quiet of the room is shattered by the sound of loud banging on my door and Layla's panicked eyes meet mine.

CHAPTER SEVENTEEN

LAYLA

*E*than hops out of bed and throws the sheet over me, ensuring I'm completely covered and then throws his boxers on.

He glances over his shoulder at me before he opens the door, and I nod my assent. He opens the door slightly, looking through the small gap, and his brows furrow in annoyance.

As soon as the door cracks open, I hear the sound of clapping and cheering, and I feel my cheeks heat in embarrassment. Ethan glances back at me, his expression now amused, and he opens the door farther so I can see Seth and Mia standing in the doorway, huge grins on their faces.

Seth thrusts a bottle of something at Ethan and exclaims, "It's about fucking time."

Mia leans forward to meet my eyes and gives me a wink. "I feel like congratulations are in order; *I* needed a cigarette after that performance."

"Oh my God!" I cry.

"Yep, that's it." She smirks at me and I pull the sheet over my head.

"Get out!" I hear laughter, followed by the sound of retreating voices.

I stay hidden under the sheet, unsure what's going on, but I soon hear Ethan returning to the room and I peek out when I hear the door close.

He kneels back on the bed and pulls the sheet away, cleaning up the combination of us that is leaking down my thighs, with a warm washcloth.

Throwing the used cloth into the dirty-clothes hamper, he settles back onto the bed, spooning me.

"That was mortifying."

"Nah, I've had to listen to them for months, it's about time I returned the favor." He kisses me just below my ear and I shiver. "Do you feel okay?"

I nod. "I feel amazing." He curls into me so every inch of our bodies are touching, from toes to head.

"Good, now get some sleep, 'cause I'm going to want to do that again, really soon."

Breakfast was quite possibly the most awkward meal ever. Well, for me, at least. Seth and Mia seemed to thoroughly enjoy themselves, rating our performance over pancakes (solid nine point five, thank you very much) and searching Amazon for earplugs, with overnight delivery. Ethan did a lot of eye rolling, but seemed perfectly content eating his food one-handed while his other remained somewhere on my body at all times.

Okay, so, that part was nice.

As I walk into my dorm room two hours later, I have to admit I'm relieved to have some time to myself. It's been a big twenty-four hours. A big week, if I'm completely honest with myself.

I still can't quite believe we're here, or how uncomplicated it's all been, and I need some time to process everything that has happened. Especially last night.

Grabbing an iced tea from the mini-fridge, I change into a pair of sleep shorts and a tank and settle on my bed ready to take a nap.

I'm exhausted, and there's a slight ache between my legs, all of which keeps last night at the forefront of my mind. I can't believe I slept with him so soon. I've gotten close to having sex a few times before but chickened out before anything could really happen, always too insecure about both myself and my relationship.

My last boyfriend, who I had met at the gym on my way out from a yoga class, hadn't helped matters when he suggested we work out together, gently telling me he knew some great exercises that would help with the cellulite on the back of my thighs. Jerk. There's *barely* a ripple, but apparently that was too much for him.

I gently told him to get lost.

Ethan makes me feel safe though, and with our history, it really isn't surprising that our relationship is rushing full steam ahead. We're probably eight years behind where we could have been, so I refuse to question the soundness of our decisions.

There is one thing causing me a tiny bit of anxiety, though, and despite trying to push it from my mind, it keeps poking me in the face, screeching *'listen to me!'*

The L-word. Ethan has said it to me every day since we confessed our feelings. He throws it around like it's candy on Halloween, and I know he believes it, but there is a tiny part of me that doubts him. And that tiny part is preventing me from saying it back.

I want to. I want to say it more than anything because I *do* love him. There's not a doubt in my mind that I do. But every time I go to open my mouth and tell him, I freeze. And I see the look in his eye. The small flash of hurt that I'm sure he thinks he's hiding, and it kills me that I can't reassure him, the way he reassures me.

Doing my best to silence my mind, I'm on the cusp of sleep, just starting to drift off when I feel an annoying tickle along the bottom of my foot. I shake it to get rid of whatever it is, when that thought permeates my almost unconscious brain and I jerk upright with a shriek.

When my heart stops pounding, and my eyes begin to focus, I see Evie kneeling at the end of my bed, laughing so hard her eyes are a watery mess.

"Why would you do that?" The only response I get is an interesting snort laugh as she collapses onto the floor, shoulders shaking.

Narrowing my eyes, I glare at her while she attempts to pull herself together.

"Feel better now?"

"Oh my God, your face, that was gold!" She crawls

into bed with me, still snickering. "Aaaaaagghh," she imitates me, waving her arms around and collapses into another fit of giggles.

"Just you wait, payback won't be pretty."

"Yeah, I'm terrified," she scoffs and rolls onto her side, so we're face to face. "So, last night, huh? I was worried sick about you, young lady."

"Oh, please. The pornographic gif you sent me when I told you I was staying over made it very clear *exactly* what you were worried about."

"Yeah, that was a good one." She grins at me before turning serious. "I guess I should be expecting a lot more sleepovers."

"Yep." I bite down on my lip to stop a goofy smile.

"We should stop by a drugstore today; you don't want to be caught empty-handed when you guys decide to sleep together. And you should make an appointment at the student health center."

"Yeah, sounds like a plan." I pause before blurting out, "Except we slept together last night."

"Get *out!*" She slaps my shoulder in surprise and I somehow grimace and laugh at the same time. "I can't believe you didn't tell me you were going to!"

"I didn't plan it, it just happened." I shake my head. Could I be more of a cliché?

"Well, how was it? I need all the details. God, I can't believe you slept with him so soon."

My brow creases at her words, a wave of embarrassment washing over me.

"No, no, no," she exclaims when she notices my expression. "I'm glad you did, I'm just surprised, that's all. It's not like you to act so impulsively, but I'm all for it."

I nod my head and consider her words. "The thing is, it didn't feel impulsive. It doesn't feel like we've only been together for six days."

"That makes sense, I think." She shrugs. "You two have this crazy long history and I guess this is a natural evolution. Plus, when you've spent ten years wanting to jump someone, it's only natural to do it as soon as you have the opportunity."

"It hasn't been ten years, jeez. Maybe, like six or seven."

"Whatever." She rolls her eyes. "So, how was it?"

"It was good. Really, really good." I blush, and her eyes widen.

"Really? God, your first time isn't supposed to be really, *really* good. I kind of hate you now."

"I mean, it hurt. When he first, you know." I scrunch my nose up remembering the pain. "Yeah, that really hurt, but he was sweet, and he didn't rush me. Then it felt good, with just a tiny edge of pain, and then it just felt good."

Our eyes meet, and we say in unison, "really, really good" and dissolve into giggles.

Sleep is forgotten, and I spend the next hour or so giving her a blow-by-blow account of last night. Pun totally intended.

We're debating going out for lunch when there's a knock on the door and Evie jumps up to see who it is.

She lets Tash in and my heart sinks a little.

I've only seen her in passing the past few weeks,

going out of my way to avoid her. I know it's ridiculous, but a part of me is annoyed at her for flirting with Ethan. Which makes no sense because Tash flirts with every hot guy. Plus, we weren't even a couple. I mean, I was dating someone else for goodness sake, and Tash didn't know about my feelings for him.

I have enough self-awareness to realize that it's jealousy. My inner witch telling me that I can't compete with Tash's lean body, or her intense green eyes and gorgeous auburn hair.

With her heart-shaped face and cupid's bow mouth, she's the epitome of what I wish I looked like, and I struggle to believe that Ethan wants me when he could have her.

Shaking myself out of my funk, and berating myself for being so juvenile, I greet her warmly.

"You guys want to go out for lunch? I feel like I haven't seen you in forever!"

Evie side-eyes me. She still hasn't entirely forgiven Tash for the ugly jab.

"Sounds good, do you wanna just hit up the dining hall? That new vegan place has an incredible pumpkin couscous salad and I've been craving one."

They both look at me as if I just declared my love for an alien species and I shrug.

"It's good!"

Evie looks at me, her eyes sparkling mischievously. "But is it *really, really good*?"

"Shut up." I snort.

Tash looks between the two of us, a wary expression on her face. "I feel like I'm missing something?"

"Nope, just ignore her." Standing up, I quickly swap my sleep shorts for a pair of yoga pants and throw on a hoodie. "Let's go."

We're headed out the door when my phone pings with a message and I read it while trying to keep up with Evie and Tash, both of whom have legs considerably longer than mine.

Ethan: I can smell you all over my sheets.

Oh, God, how can eight words from him make my face flame like this?

Ethan: I love it when you blush.

I look around as though I'm going to find him standing next to me, but he's nowhere in sight and I sigh in exasperation. While I'm considering how to respond, my phone goes off again.

Ethan: Where are you?

Me: Headed to the dining hall. Wanna catch up later?

. . .

I get no response, so I shove my phone back in the pocket of my hoodie and hurry to catch up with the others.

Twenty minutes later, we're seated at a table in the quiet dining hall when I feel the hairs on the back of my neck stand on end.

Tash, who is sitting across from me, looks up to my right and a slow, lazy smile spreads across her face. She starts twirling a lock of hair around her finger and tilts her head in a way that can only be described as coquettish.

Lord, this girl could give lessons on flirting.

I know he's coming before I see him, and despite this, I still jump when he appears behind me and his fingers squeeze my ribcage and tickle.

"Aaah! Don't do that!" I duck my head down in embarrassment and do a quick check to make sure no one heard my squeal, while Ethan chuckles beside me.

He turns his attention to Evie, who is sitting beside me, and slides her chair around to the end of the table and pulls another chair up to the table and takes a seat.

"You don't mind, right?" he throws out.

"Jesus, too bad if I did, I guess," she throws right back, and I smile, watching their back and forth.

I glance over at Tash and see her watching the three of us with surprise. I don't have time to worry about it because before I can make sense of what is happening, my face is in Ethan's hands, my mouth is pressed against his and my mind empties of every thought except how good his tongue feels sliding against mine.

He pulls back ever so slightly, his lips still resting on mine and I feel them twist up in a smile.

"Hi."

"Hey."

He brushes another soft kiss across my mouth, then turns to look at the plate in front of me with a look of disgust.

"What is that?" His voice completely horrified I take advantage of his distraction to chance a look at Tash and see her staring at Ethan, wide-eyed and mouth agape. I can't help the small sliver of satisfaction that I feel.

"Pumpkin couscous salad. You want some?" I offer up a heaping forkful to him with a quirked eyebrow.

"Fuck, no." He pushes away from the table noisily. "I'll be back."

I watch him walk away, admiring his butt as he goes. It's a really nice butt.

"I'm just running to the bathroom." Evie swallows the last of her mac and cheese and follows in the same direction Ethan just headed.

As soon as she's gone, the air shifts and I feel the tension pulsing between Tash and me. I choose to ignore it and dig back into my salad, hopeful that Ethan and Evie return quickly.

"So, you and Ethan, huh?" Her voice is slightly higher pitched than normal.

"Uh, yeah, it's pretty new."

"I thought you were dating Michael?" I hear a note of accusation, but I'm not sure if I'm imagining it, and, for the first time, it hits me how bad this looks.

Jumping straight from Michael to Ethan. I've been in my own little happy bubble for the past week, surrounded by people who knew our story and were happy for us. I had almost convinced myself that Michael was just a bad dream.

"We broke up. We were never serious though." I hate the defensiveness in my voice.

"Right." She takes a sip of her water, her eyes sizing me up. "Well, I'm happy for you. He's a good guy, and I knew he had feelings for you."

"Thanks, I really do appreciate that. I would hate for there to be any awkwardness between us."

"Oh God, no. No awkwardness. Although, you know…" She looks at me reproachfully. "If you had told me you were interested, I never would have flirted with him. I would have just let you have him."

I ignore the twinge of annoyance I feel at her insinuation that I needed her to step aside. I ignore the desire to yell at her that he wanted me, even when he could have had her. I even ignore the impulse to poke my tongue out at her.

Instead, I take the high road. "It was a confusing situation. But thank you, that means a lot."

She reaches across the table and takes my hand, squeezing it gently, and smiles at me. Her genuine smile. The one that lights up her face and reminds me why we're friends.

"I really am happy for you, Lay. You deserve a good guy, and I think you two make a great pair."

"What about you, who are you see—" My phone starts vibrating across the table, interrupting me, and my heart does a happy flip when I see my sister's name on the screen.

I turn to Tash. "I'm so sorry, it's my sister."

She waves me off. "Take it, don't even worry."

"Hey, CJ, what's up?"

"Bubs! You free next Saturday?"

"I think so, why?" Knowing my sister, I'm almost scared to ask.

"Girls' night, baby girl. Girls'. Night!"

CHAPTER EIGHTEEN

ETHAN

*T*he locker room is humid and a thin sheen of sweat sticks to my skin. Seth is beside me bullshitting on about something, but all I can hear is Bradshaw's voice, bragging about some girl he nailed last night.

The fucker makes my skin crawl.

"She moaned like a bitch porn star when I stuffed her with my cock."

I've replayed those words over in my mind a million times since he spat them at me last week. Every time I do, I relive the satisfaction of his bone-crunching beneath my knuckles and feel the itch to do it all over again.

"Dickhole, are you even listening to me?"

"What?" I slam my locker shut and sit down to lace up my Converse, trying to concentrate on Seth's voice.

"You and Layla coming to *Hound Dog* to celebrate?"

I roll my shoulders and consider his question. I don't really feel like I have anything to celebrate. It was a close game, and the guys did a great job to pull out a touchdown in the last three minutes, giving us a two-point win against our biggest rival. I, however, had nothing to do with the win and my ass spent the game warming the bench.

"Nah, Layla's going out with her sister tonight and I agreed to have dinner with my dad."

Seth's eyes light up at the mention of Jackson Miller, the way most football fans do, and if I was in a better mood, I would invite him to join us. But after receiving a two-game suspension earlier this week for aggressive behavior, I know I'm about to get my ass handed to me, and I'd prefer not to have an audience for it.

"Okay, cool. We'll catch you at home then." He gives me a knowing look and slaps me on my back before making his way out of the locker room, shouting out goodbyes and joking around with our teammates the entire way.

Sighing, I stand up and roughly run my towel over my still-damp hair. No one will be joking around with me anytime soon, they're all still pissy about me knocking out their captain. It turns out no matter how much of a douche he is, the team doesn't appreciate the new guy putting him on his ass in front of a roomful of jocks and sorority skanks.

I throw my bag over my shoulder and after giving a quick goodbye to the few guys not hanging on Brad-shaw's every word, I head out through the tunnel that leads directly to the parking lot.

My night starts to look up when I spot Layla

standing at the end of the walkway, a huge smile on her face, talking to my parents, her arms wrapped around Emme's shoulders.

There's a selfish part of me that hopes she's blowing off her plans for tonight to be a buffer between my dad and me.

"Ethan!" Emme's voice is a screech as she breaks away from Layla, running at full speed and throwing herself into my arms.

"Hey, Oops." I wrap my arms around her and let myself savor this brief moment of adoration.

She pulls back slightly until she's looking me in the eye. "Why didn't you play today? It's *so* boring when you don't play!"

I meet my father's sardonic expression over Emme's shoulder and grimace slightly.

"Alright, Miss Emmerson, if you want to get to your sleepover in time, we need to leave now," my mom interrupts.

"Oh, yay! I'm sleeping over at Meg's tonight." Emme leans in to whisper in my ear. "We're gonna stay up all night, but don't tell Mom, okay?"

"Promise."

She plants a loud kiss on my cheek and jumps down.

"You two come for brunch tomorrow. No excuses." My mom hugs me close. "I'm so happy you two finally got your act together." Her voice is low so only I can hear her, and my gaze cuts to Layla who is standing back watching us with a look of happiness on her face.

"Me too."

After a protracted round of goodbyes where Emme hugs and kisses each of us multiple times, it's finally just my father, Layla, and I standing there.

The rest of the team has started to trickle out and I notice the side looks and double takes when they notice my dad. Layla picks up on the shift in my mood and presses her body close against mine, stretching up and kissing my jaw.

"Hey."

"Hi." My voice is raspy, and I pull her in tight, still not quite believing that I'm finally allowed to touch her like this.

An awkward cough distracts us both and Layla steps away, her cheeks burning and my body already missing the comfort of hers.

"Are you joining us tonight, Layla? You're more than welcome." My father's eyes are warm and his invitation sincere.

"Uh, I can." She quirks an eyebrow at me in question and despite how badly I want her there tonight, I know how much she's looking forward to going out.

"No, she can't, Dad. She's going out with Cassidy tonight."

"Oh, well, that's a shame, but I'm sure you'll have much more fun with your sister." He chuckles. "And I'll make sure Ethan has bail money set aside, just in case."

Layla giggles. "Oh God, my parents would kill her if they ever got that phone call again." She pulls her phone out and checks the time. "Okay, I have to head off then. You guys have a great time and—" she turns to me, wrapping her arms around my waist, "—I'll message you later."

"Yeah, do that." I lean down until my mouth brushes against hers and I steal a taste. "Definitely do that."

"See you later, Mr. Miller." She throws him a wave and my dad smiles at her indulgently.

"Goodbye, Layla."

I watch her walk away, enjoying the sway of her rounded ass, while Dad surreptitiously checks his phone.

"You ready?"

"Yeah, let's get out of here."

I lead the way to my truck and we make our way to his favorite Italian restaurant, indulging in idle chit-chat while I fantasize about the giant bowl of pasta I'm about to devour.

All the casual back and forth lulls me into a false sense of security, and by the time the waitress brings our food to the table, I'm almost convinced Dad is going to let my transgression slide.

Just as I'm about to dig into my spaghetti bolognese, his voice pulls me up short.

"A two-game suspension, Ethan, really?" My hands tighten around my cutlery.

"I'm not going to apologize, Dad. The guy's an asshole and he deserved worse than what he got."

"I don't doubt that he did, but you need to think about the team. The team always has to come first, son."

"Fuck the team, Dad. Fuck them." My entire body is

tense, and I can feel an angry pulse start to beat in my temple.

He glares at me across the table and I can see his jaw clenching. This goes against his entire ethos for life. I know my father loves us, but I also know his team will always come first. He doesn't know any other way, a fact which has been proven time and again. You would think when he retired from the Giants, it would have been our turn. Instead, he accepted an offensive coordinator position with them and they remained priority number one.

I won't live that way. A team will never mean more to me than the individuals I love.

"You committed to this team, Ethan. You owe them more than this."

I slam my cutlery down, drawing a few glances from nearby diners, but I couldn't care less.

"I owe them *shit*, Dad. I never asked to be on the team, you did that. *You* pulled fucking strings I never wanted you to pull and left me with no choice but to say yes."

He looks completely taken aback by my response. "You were playing football in Washington, you're telling me you weren't going to play when you came home?" His tone is defensive, but I can't bring myself to give a fuck. This is a conversation we should have had a long time ago.

"That's exactly what I'm saying. I had no intention of trying out for the team. I came back here to sort things out with Layla and finish my degree, that's it.

Why the hell would I force my way onto an established team when I really couldn't care less about football?"

"Don't be ridiculous, of course you care about football, you led your high school team to the championship twice. I was there, I saw how much the game meant to you. If it didn't, why would you have gone on to play at WSU?"

I exhale harshly, contemplating his question. Because, despite his defensiveness, he has a point. I do enjoy football, but it was never the all-encompassing passion that he feels.

I lean back in my chair. "I played at WSU because I could just enjoy the game. There was no pressure. Do you have any fucking idea how hard it is being your son and living up to those expectations?" He starts to talk, but I cut him off. "Do you know what it's like to feel the weight of disappointment crushing you because your father is a football champion and you don't want to follow in his footsteps?"

"Now, stop right there." He points at me angrily. "I have never, not for one single second, been disappointed in you. It's just—" he runs a hand haphazardly through his hair, "—you could have been great."

"I am going to be great. Hell, I *am* great, but at something I actually give a fuck about, and that's architecture, not football." I sigh. "I'm okay with that, Dad. Now you need to be, too." He deflates in front of me. "I was always upfront with you. I told you that football was never going to be my path, it's about time you realize I mean it."

He nods his head solemnly and continues to stare at me, almost as though he's seeing me for the first time.

"Do you really think you disappoint me?"

I look up and meet eyes that are eerily similar to my own. "How could you not be?"

"Then I really fucked up this parenting gig." My father shakes his head in defeat. "From the moment you were old enough to know your own mind, you followed it. You knew what you wanted and never gave up until you got it. I have nothing but respect for the man you are, and I will never, *never*, be disappointed in you, or the choices you make, do you understand me?"

I nod mutely.

"Right, now let's eat before our food gets any colder."

His voice leaves no room for argument and we both turn our attention to the food in front of us, eating in awkward silence.

The night doesn't improve, the air remains uncomfortable and as I head home after dropping my father off, I'm still trying to process everything that was said.

Pulling into the apartment complex's parking lot my phone goes off. I slide the gears into park and pull it out, relief coursing through me when I see Layla's name.

Layla: Booty call? 😉

CHAPTER NINETEEN

LAYLA

A smile plays across my lips as I watch my sister climb up on the bar with a group of strangers and proceed to give the entire crowd a rousing rendition of "Wannabe" by the Spice Girls. Even funnier is when she attempts to drag her best friends, Skye and Wyatt, up with her. They both give in, Skye easily and Wyatt begrudgingly, because we all know there's no point in saying no to Cassidy. She is a giant ball of crazy who will not be denied.

I observe the crowd, cradling the same Moscato I've had for the last hour, and marvel at the way everyone's eyes follow every move CJ makes. She glows when the limelight is shone on her. Always has, and as much as I love her, it was difficult at times, growing up in that shadow.

"Your sister might possibly be the craziest person I've ever met," Mason declares playfully, pulling out a chair and taking a seat next to me.

I duck my head and take a sip of my wine for

courage. Cassidy's new boyfriend is hot. Capital H. Capital O. Capital T.

Nerves under control, I glance up and see him, gaze locked on my sister and an indulgent smile plastered on his face. He looks like a man in love.

"Yep, she's a handful alright." I consider him thoughtfully. "But she's worth every single moment of chaos." I shake my head. I can't explain why, but the need for him to know this strikes me suddenly and determinedly. "Loving her isn't always easy, but there's no one who's worth it more than CJ. No one."

He turns to face me, all trace of humor gone. "I realize this more and more, every day. These last few months, she's changed my life and I know I'm a lucky son of a bitch." He shrugs. "Even if loving her wasn't worth it, I don't think I could stop."

Well, I'll be a son of a monkey. Lifting the glass to my lips, I point to him. "I think I like you."

Our laughter is interrupted by the sound of Cassidy calling out to the crowd as she scans the faces around her.

"Layla! Bubs! Where are you? Get your cute ass up heeeere!"

Mason quirks an eyebrow at me. "I think that's your cue."

I take my phone out of my purse and pull up the Uber app. "My cue to leave? Why, yes. Yes, it is."

After organizing my ride, I shoot off a quick text to Ethan and turn back to Mason.

"Will you let the others know I said goodbye?"

"Are you okay getting home?" he questions, his voice conveying concern.

Yeah, I definitely like this guy.

My back is slammed against the wall, hips holding me in place and a huge hard-on pressed against my belly.

"I missed you."

I smile against his lips. Hello, Captain Obvious.

"You don't say?"

He's staring down at me with an expression I can't quite pinpoint, except to say I want his eyes on me like this always. Could quite possibly *need* them on me, inciting this anarchy of emotion, where my heart betrays my head so rapturously. Because as his eyes meet mine, in this moment, I feel beautiful, and no matter how fleeting it is, I'm going to cherish this feeling.

Ethan bites his full bottom lip before a slow, lazy smile spreads across his face, highlighting the dimples I love so much.

"Why don't you take me to your room, and you can show me how much you missed me?" I lean up and place an open-mouthed kiss on his neck, sucking slightly, oddly turned on by the thought of my mark on his body.

"Seth and Mia aren't here, why limit ourselves to the bedroom?"

My gaze flies to meet his, and he stares back at me, a teasing glint in his eye.

"Uh, no. I don't need your roommates walking in on us, being scarred by the sight of my naked butt. To the bedroom, Millhouse!" I try to push off the wall, but he holds me tight.

"C'mon, Lay." He leans down, and his breath caresses my ear as his whisper coaxes, "Be brave with me."

A shiver runs down my spine, and I'm pretty sure my eyes are glazed and lust drunk.

"'Kay."

His hands slide down my body, his fingertips firing every synapse along my skin until they land on my butt and squeeze. A moan I'm helpless to stop escapes, and I feel him jerk against my stomach.

His mouth lands on mine as he simultaneously lifts me up and wraps my legs around his waist. When his tongue slips into my mouth, I thread my hands through his hair and try to pull him closer. The sensation of his tongue tasting mine, wrestling fervently, is heady and overwhelming and we continue the erotic dance as he walks us into the living area, and we fall back onto the sofa. I straddle his lap and when my white dress rides up my thighs, I notice its bright contrast to my tanned skin and his black jeans. Jeans that are roughly rubbing against my clit, causing me to move involuntarily.

Rolling my hips, Ethan exhales harshly and his hands claw at my ass. "Again, Layla."

I recreate the movement, with a little less poise this time and I feel him grow even harder beneath me, the need for contact is now overpowering. My breathing is erratic and while his hands and mouth explore every inch of me, I fumble with his zipper, desperate to free him and get him inside of me. My hands are almost frantic when I feel him chuckle against my skin.

"You want my dick, baby?"

My breath hitches in surprise when a finger pulls my panties aside and slides along my slit. I'm so wet, and his hand feels so freaking good, my legs begin to shake. The moment his finger makes contact with my clit, I gasp, and he takes advantage of this, his mouth moving back over mine.

He circles my clit, and his tongue slides against mine, mimicking the movement of his finger. I feel myself sink deeper into him, on the edge of an orgasm that's threatening an intensity I would be anxious about if I was more coherent.

Suddenly his finger and tongue are gone, and I'm left feeling empty. And annoyed.

"Why did you stop?"

He smirks at the aggression in my voice. "Undo me."

I want to tell him off for being so bossy, but more than that I want to get back to the touching and the loving.

Also, the coming. I definitely want to make the coming happen.

Groaning, my hands go back to his zipper and while I slowly pull it down, his hands move to the spaghetti straps of my dress, sliding them down my arms. His fingers tease a path down my skin until they meet my pebbled nipples. I momentarily forget where I am and what I'm doing as the sensation of him grazing, stroking, and pinching overcomes me.

He roughly pulls down the top of my dress, exposing my entire breasts, and the warm suction of his mouth engulfs me.

"Layla." He pulls back ever so slightly, just enough that I can still feel his lips move against my skin. "Undo me. My dick needs to come home."

My hands get back to business and in seconds I'm freeing him, eye to eye with what is fast becoming my favorite part of his body.

He lifts his hips and I pull his jeans and boxer briefs down before I seal my mouth back to his. Grasping his face in both hands, I nibble along his bottom lip and his hand nudges my butt up, so I'm kneeling, hovering above him. I break our connection to watch as he takes hold of himself and impatiently pumps a few times, his face a study in concentration. I blush slightly at the sight of his penis, all red and angry-looking, as though it's enraged it's not yet inside me. Yeah, well, that makes two of us, buddy.

"Panties off, Bug." His voice is commanding in a way I haven't heard before and I immediately rush to slip them down my thighs and pull them off entirely, squealing quietly when I almost fall back in my eagerness. But Ethan's reflexes are on point, steadying me before I even register what almost happened.

"Hold up your dress, I want to watch." Again, I follow his orders with no compunction.

He keeps a bracing hand on my thigh, pulling me down so I'm close enough for him to run the head of his erection through my slit. My balance falters when his crown makes contact with my swollen clit and I grab onto his shoulders to stabilize myself and word-lessly slide down until my hips meet his.

"Fuuuuuck." The word is a slow hiss. His hands find my hips, holding me with a grip that verges on painful and his eyes glued to where we're joined.

His mouth finds my neck, licking and sucking, biting and kissing, when I start to move experimen-tally, rolling my hips back and forth, then circling them around, to see what feels better. Turns out, it all feels good.

I pick up the pace, and these ridiculous mewls I can't seem to control, keep bursting out of me.

"Shit, that feels so fucking good, baby." He grasps my breasts and squeezes before tweaking my nipples, harshly. The stab of pain shoots straight down to my clit and spurs me on. "Your tits look amazing, bouncing like that while you ride me. Jesus Christ, Layla, you like riding my cock, baby?"

"So good, *so good*. It's so fucking good," I grate out.

His hand finds my clit and I start bouncing up and down, chasing the orgasm that's so close I can almost taste it. I'm practically twerking on his dick right now, and if I had any self-awareness left, I would probably be mortified. But I don't, not one tiny ounce, so I continue to twerk until the orgasm explodes through me. My body stiffens, and white dots cloud my vision before I finally collapse forward, my head falling into the crook of his neck.

Ethan wraps his arms tight around my waist, nuzzling my neck and he starts thrusting up, hard and erratic.

The room is silent except for the loud grunts Ethan is making with each thrust, and the sound of our bodies slapping together. It's all so wonderfully lewd and dirty. I kind of love it.

I turn my head and my lips meet the shell of Ethan's ear. Taking a deep fortifying breath, I gather all my courage, ready to try something I never thought I would.

"I love it when you fuck my pussy this hard," I whisper. "The way it sounds when your cock slams into me, all covered in my cum. Don't stop, Ethan, you need to go harder. *Please*." My voice is needy, desperate almost, and a loud roar echoes around the room as he thrusts up one final time, seating himself fully before coming hard and fast.

We fall back onto the sofa, clinging onto each other, all sweaty and slippery; exhausted and sated. His hands continue to run over my body, chasing away the slight chill from the cold air hitting my clammy skin.

My head still in the clouds, it takes a moment for me to realize his shoulders are shaking beneath me.

"What are you laughing at?" I ask lazily, my body still pressed against him, a tired achiness seeping through me.

"Holy fuck, that was some damn good dirty talk. I think my dick might have superpowers."

I roll my eyes. It's behind my closed lids, but it totally still counts. "You give your penis way too much credit."

CHAPTER TWENTY

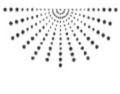

ETHAN

"*I* fucking love Thanksgiving." Taking one hand off the steering wheel, I start counting off items. "Turkey, stuffing, green bean casserole, oh God, my mom's green bean casserole." My eyes roll back in undisguised bliss at the thought of it. "*Plus,* pumpkin pie and permission to sit on my ass all day watching football. It's basically the perfect day."

"So, your idea of a perfect day is pretty much stuffing your face and sitting on your butt?" Layla giggles. "Good to know you're so easily pleased."

My hand finds her thigh and squeezes. "Well, there's a couple of other things you can add to that list." I throw her a salacious wink and delight in the way her nose scrunches up in disgust.

"Noted," she replies wryly, before changing the subject. "It was so nice of your parents to invite all of us for dinner. I think having Thanksgiving at home would have upset CJ even more."

"You think it's really over with her boyfriend?"

Pulling up at a red light, I turn to face her. "It sounded like she was really into him."

"She was, and I think that's the problem. I'm hoping she just needs some time to work through everything and then she'll come to her senses. I really think he's a good guy, she just needs to hear him out."

We take off again and spend the last few minutes of the drive chatting about the rest of our Thanksgiving weekend plans, and as we pull into my parents' drive-way, I decide to ask her the question I've been wanting to ask for days.

"So, Seth and Mia aren't coming back until Sunday night, why don't you spend the weekend at my place?" I expect hesitation, and I'm fucking thrilled when she doesn't even blink at my suggestion.

"Yeah, that sounds good. Evie isn't back unt—" She's cut off by loud excited screeches and feet storming down the path.

I climb out of my truck expecting to see Emme running toward us, but instead, I see her trailing behind Cassidy, who is racing to Layla. Pulling up short, just in front of Lay, she turns around and does some weird little dance, shouting, "Winner, winner, chicken dinner." She points to Emme with a huge smile on her face. "You need to work on your speed, Nugget."

Emme stands with her arms crossed over her chest and a cute little scowl on her face. "You need to learn how to win more grayshly, CJ."

"I think you mean, graciously, kid, and you'll find I do very little with grace." She shrugs, turning to Layla and folds her into a giant hug. I watch as they have a whispered conversation and note how tired Cassidy looks.

Clapping my hands loudly, I rub them together to ward off the chill. "Right, there's food to be eaten and football to be watched, so let's get our asses inside, out of the cold."

We make our way in and are warmly greeted by both of our mothers who are bustling around the kitchen, doing who the hell knows what, before Emme drags Layla and Cassidy to her room, to show off the new catcher's mitt Dad bought her.

"Dinner will be ready in half an hour, Emmerson, so don't go too far," my mother calls after them.

I grab a spoon and scoop up a small amount of cream from the bowl Layla's mom is whipping.

"Hey!" She smacks my hand. "Hands off, mister. You know." She eyes me suspiciously. "The cream isn't the only thing I should be telling you to keep your hands off."

My mother snorts in the background and I feel my face heat in a manner I'm very unaccustomed to.

"Consider yourself warned, okay? I'd hate to put my knife skills to the test, got it?"

My mind immediately replays the events of this morning when my hands were very much *not* kept to myself. "Got it." I salute her jokingly and lean in to place a kiss on her cheek.

"Good, because my baby thinks you're the bomb diggity and I'd hate to have to hurt you."

I chuckle at her turn of phrase. Laura Jensen is a low-key goofball. I see a lot of her in Layla, although I would never admit that to her. I don't have a death wish.

"Christ, Laura, did we timewarp back to the nineties? No one says bomb diggity anymore." My mother taps her cheek. "How about planting one of those kisses on your mother's cheek, huh?"

I do as I'm told, wrapping her up in a tight hug while Laura answers indignantly.

"It's making a comeback, Annie, just you watch."

"Anyway," I interrupt. "Shouldn't I be having this conversation with Mr. Jensen? Isn't the dad the one I'm supposed to be terrified of?"

"Oh please," she scoffs. "We all know William thinks the sun shines out of your ass. He's probably had this conversation with Layla, warning *her* not to hurt *you!*"

I spend the next few minutes loitering in the kitchen, trying to go unnoticed while stealing scraps of food, and marveling at how good it feels being wrapped up in the warmth of a combined Miller/Jensen celebration.

When we moved here all those years ago, our mothers immediately bonded, and with Layla and I becoming fast friends, we spent most of our time in each other's homes until it eventually felt like we were one big extended family. Although, I guess it was more like a weird incestuous kind of family, where the brother and sister want to bone each other. Okay, so maybe that's not the best analogy after all.

"Ethan James Miller!" I'm snapped out of my thoughts by my mother's cross tone. "Stop stealing food. Get out of here and go join your father and William in the theater room."

I hold my hands up in surrender. "Okay, jeez, relax," I placate her before my hand shoots out, and I grab a bread roll from the plate in front of me, with what I hope is an endearing smirk.

"Go!" she yells. I guess not so much.

I blow her a kiss and make my way to the theater room, prepared to settle in for an afternoon of football. As I walk down the hallway lined with framed family pictures, I stop in surprise when I see a new addition.

It's an old snapshot. I'm probably about seven or eight years old, and Layla and I are sitting out on the large veranda of our craftsman home. She's staring at a flower in her hands and I'm staring at her. Both of our expressions are filled with wonder, as though we can't quite comprehend the beauty of what's right in front of us.

Fuck, I never even had a chance, I think, and make a mental note to ask my mom if I can get a copy of the picture.

The next few hours are spent enjoying the people I love the most. We eat, we laugh, we love and it's the best Thanksgiving I can remember. Everyone seems to have taken the news of our relationship in their stride, and there's no weirdness when my hands end up on her, despite Laura's warnings. Which is good because even if it's an innocent arm stretched along the back of her chair, fingers playing with her hair, I find I can't *not* touch her when she's near me.

The only drawback to the day is Cassidy's despondency. She does her best to put on a brave face and appear unaffected, but she's obviously miserable. I really hope she works things out with her guy.

After dinner is finished, we all head in different directions. The men settle back in front of the television, our mothers head to the living room armed with coffee and Emme runs to her room, in what I'm sure is a clandestine attempt to watch rot-your-brain shows on her tablet.

Layla and Cassidy sneak outside, and as much as I want to follow her out there, the expression on their faces makes it clear that's probably not a good idea.

An hour later, they still haven't returned and I'm craving a Layla-fix, so, deciding they've had plenty of alone time, I head out in search of them.

I follow the sound of hushed tones down the hallway that leads to the front porch, but just as I'm about to open the door and make my presence known, the sound of Layla's voice, filled with anxiety, stops me.

"He explained what happened. He won't disappear again, he promised."

A derisive snort assaults my ears. "Of course, that's what he'd say. But what if it gets too hard again? What if you start fighting and suddenly it's not all sex and fun? From what you told me, he ran away because loving you was too hard, and he couldn't handle it. Well, guess what? Love is fucking hard and if he couldn't handle it then, how do you know he can handle it now? How do you know in six months' time you won't be on the phone to me, crying your eyes out because he's ghosted you again?"

What the actual fuck? Cassidy's voice is brittle and harsh, holding none of her usual warmth. My hand tightens around the doorknob I'm still holding, and I try to talk myself out of barging out there and confronting her. Until the next words out of her mouth take hold of my heart and squeeze until the physical pain makes any movement impossible.

"You were broken, Layla. *He* did that to you, and he did it with no warning, no explanation and honestly, he has no real defense. I understand you wanting to hold on to the friendship and trying to work that out, but I have no fucking clue why you would ever hand your heart over to him. It'll only get crushed again."

I risk leaning forward, looking for a glimpse of Layla, but as soon as my eyes land on her, I wish I hadn't. Her face is creased with worry, and her eyes blaze with confusion.

Taking a step back, I scrub my hands over my face, my own confusion causing a war to rage within myself. Finally, deciding this isn't a conversation we should have when we're both so emotional, I turn and walk inside, nervous, for the first time since my mouth had tasted hers.

❧

The sound of my keys landing on the kitchen counter echoes around the room. We barely spoke on the drive home. In fact, Layla has said very little since re-entering my family home a couple of hours ago.

I can see Cassidy's words have sent her crawling

into herself. I see her internal struggle as she tries to convince herself I'm worth the risk. Now, I just need to figure out a way to make her see that being with me is no risk at all.

Layla moves to the fridge, stocking it with all the leftovers my mom insisted we bring home.

"It looks like we'll be eating pretty well for the next few days," I say, coming up behind her, taking a moment to admire her ass as she's bent over, placing cartons on the shelves.

"What?" She stands back up, her voice distracted.

I pull her back into me and wrap my arms around her, kissing her lightly in the crook of her neck and repeat myself.

"Oh." She pulls away and moves to the other side of the kitchen, putting as much distance between us as possible. "Yeah, I guess so." A forced smile crosses her face.

"Are you okay?" I'm aware I'm leading her, but we need to talk about this and I know her first instinct is to run from any kind of confrontation.

"Mmm-hmm." She nods. "I'm fine. But I'm tired, so I think I'm going to head to bed."

"I heard you and Cassidy," I blurt out. She stills, and her face crumples. For a moment I think she's going to cry and a flash of panic shoots through me. But she takes a deep, calming breath and lifts her head to look me straight in the eye.

"You left me."

"I did," I reply, nodding my head.

"I don't understand how you could have left me so easily." She takes a step toward me, but catches herself and presses her back against the wall, as though she needs a physical anchor to keep away from me. "You were my best friend and you say you loved me, but if that was true how could you just cut me out of your life like that? You made me feel like I was nothing, like our entire friendship had been a complete lie." Her shoulders slump slightly, and I have to use every ounce of my willpower to hold my position next to the refrigerator, to give her the space I know she needs to have this conversation.

"Our friendship wasn't a lie, Bug." Her eyes close at the use of her nickname, and I drag my hand through my hair, frustrated. "I explained this. I thought you understood."

Her eyes flash, and I realize that was the wrong thing to say.

"You know what I understand?" she rushes on, not giving me a chance to answer. "I understand that I spent four years of high school listening to girls talk about how hot you were, how badly they wanted to date you, *God*." She flinches. "I listened to endless conversations about what a good *fuck* you were!" Her voice breaks, and I instinctively move toward her, but she stops me with the raise of her hand. "I would have put up with all of that, *all of it*, to have you in my life. That's how important *you* were to *me*."

She pushes off the wall and stalks toward the bedroom. I follow close behind, determined to have my say.

"Okay, first, I never fucked anyone in high school, so anything you heard was complete bullshit."

I see her shoulders shake and hear a quiet derisive laugh. "Yeah, because that's the takeaway from what I just said. It doesn't matter if it wasn't true. *I still had to hear it.*"

We both storm into my bedroom and I watch in shock when she starts gathering up her things and throwing them into her backpack.

"Wait, what are you doing?" I grab her arm as she rushes past me, turning her around to face me. "So, one conversation with your sister and you're done? Cassidy decides I can't be trusted, so you're ready to walk away? Because Cassidy doesn't know shit about me. I was a dumbass punk." I move closer to her and she remains still, providing me with some hope that I can still save this. "I was eighteen and couldn't handle the reality of never having you. Of watching you fall in love with some asshole loser, and it made me do something stupid. But I did it to protect myself, not to hurt you." I move away and start pacing the room, memories of that first year overwhelming me. "*Nothing* about leaving you was easy, Layla. It fucking killed me."

My voice is harsh, full of anguish, and she approaches from behind, running a calming hand down my arm before she steps in front of me, wrapping me in a hug. I return her embrace with fervor; grateful she's heard what I said. I lean into her, inhaling the strawberry scent of her shampoo and my lips find her neck, placing soft kisses just below her ear.

She stiffens under my touch and moves her hands up to my chest, pushing back slightly.

"I think, maybe, we rushed into this too quickly." Her eyes are filled with sadness and I shake my head in denial.

"No, rushing in is the opposite of what we did. We couldn't have possibly gone any slower. We fucking turtled into this relationship."

A wistful smile plays across her lips. "Did you just turn turtle into a verb?"

I pull her closer to me, tightening my grip in a desperate attempt to stop her from slipping away.

"I love you."

She closes her eyes and pulls my head down until my forehead rests against hers. "I know you do, but I need some time to think." Her lips brush along mine, a gentle whisper I barely feel. "I'm sorry."

CHAPTER TWENTY-ONE

LAYLA

I trail my finger along the row of books, my eyes searching the titles for the one I need. Pushing my glasses up on my nose, I exhale a small sigh of frustration. It really shouldn't be this hard to find a stupid book, but my head is all over the place, just as it has been for the past week.

Since the moment Ethan dropped me back at the dorm last week, the only thing I've been able to think about is our relationship. I spent the rest of the Thanksgiving weekend holed up in my room, crying, binge-watching *The Office* and replaying Cassidy's words over in my head.

When Evie returned on Sunday afternoon, she found me in bed, tearstained and cradling a sweater that Ethan had forgotten. It took a few hours and a few shots of vodka for her to get the story out of me and afterward, much to my disgust, Evie remained firmly entrenched in Team Ethan, urging me to see him and work things out face to face. But I'm just not ready, yet.

Ethan and I have been messaging daily, and I've assured him that we're not over, that I'm not ending anything, I just need some time to work through my feelings. He's frustrated and angry, but he's giving me the space I need.

Letting out a little squeak of relief, I finally spot the textbook I need and pull it from the shelf. I turn to head back to my workstation when I remember the librarian's reminder, that the latest book from my favorite author had just been stocked.

Turning around, I weave my way through the library stacks until I end up in the correct area and find myself, once again, searching through titles.

My finger traces the spines, looking for the familiar name when I hear footsteps approaching in the next stack over, and a familiar voice whispering.

"Oh my God, April, you have no idea. I've never had a guy talk to me like that before. That motherfucker deserves a degree in dirty talk."

I peek through the shelving and spot Tash. She's talking to a girl who I can't place but is vaguely familiar, and she has a smug smile plastered over her face.

I feel a small answering smile tilt my own lips. I'm happy she's found someone she likes. Despite a propensity to be slightly shallow, she is a nice person, and I want her to be happy.

Spotting my book, I grab it off the shelf and begin to move away, not wanting to eavesdrop further and invade Tash's privacy. I've taken a few steps when I hear words that cause me to stop in my tracks, and the blood to rush to my head.

"I swear, I was about to give up, but Ethan was definitely worth the wait."

The other girl giggles at Tash's declaration. "I can't believe he slept with you, I thought he was all about that nerd girl."

"Ugh, Princess Von Boring? It's so sad, she's into him so much and I think he just feels sorry for her, you know? He's too nice for his own good."

She pauses, and I know I should leave. That I need to force my feet to move so I don't hear anything else that will punch another hole in my heart. But I can't, and I stay locked in place, Tash's words infiltrating every doubt I ever had about my relationship with Ethan.

She lowers her voice even more before continuing. "He had to come back home for family reasons, and she just assumed he came back for her." My eyes are helpless to stop watching this train wreck and I see her friend nod as though it all makes complete sense.

"He's such a sweet guy and he doesn't want to hurt her, but really? I mean how could she ever imagine he would want her when he could have me?"

The contemptuous tone in her voice snaps me out of my paralysis, and as every conversation I've overheard over the years, and every sentiment that echoed Tash's, attempts to force its way front and center, Ethan's voice overpowers them all.

"She's a bitch, Bug. A complete bitch."

Memories chase me, and I realize that despite what I just heard, despite the hundreds of cruel comments I've ever overheard, Ethan has never lied to me. He's never given me any reason to doubt his word. I've let conversations like this change the course of our relationship before and I won't do it again. I race to gather my things and head for the exit, finally sure of what I need to do.

Four years earlier...

"Are you ready for exams?"

I grimace exaggeratedly in response to Renee's question and she laughs softly. The sound of the rushing water we're using to wash our paintbrushes almost drowns out the delicate sound.

The art studio is quiet, the rest of the class having hurried out as soon as the bell rang, eager to rush to the cafeteria, or football field, or wherever it is they spend their lunch period. Renee and I are the only ones left, dutifully cleaning our tools while we gossip about everything going on in our lives.

"Did you hear Taylor Swift is touring next year? I really hope I can get tickets."

"Oh God, me too. I would love to see her live. Even more than that, I'd love to drag Ethan to a concert, just to annoy him." We dissolve into giggles at the thought until the sound of the classroom door opening silences us.

We're down in the back of the studio, hidden behind a nib wall that holds the sinks. I peek around the wall and turning back to Renee, I roll my eyes and mouth, *"Jasmine and Kelly."*

"Ugh, just hurry up and find it, I need to get to the cafeteria." Jasmine's nasal voice rings throughout the room.

"God, calm down, Jazz. You don't even know if Ethan is in there."

The mention of Ethan's name causes me to freeze and I can see Renee out of the corner of my eye, watching me worriedly.

"Levi messaged me and told me he's there, so get your ass into gear, I have to get there and work my magic."

There's a moment of silence, only broken by the sound of papers shuffling and tools colliding, before Kelly retorts, *"I don't know why you're bothering, everyone knows he's going to prom with Layla the loser."*

A small gasp escapes me, and I close my eyes tight, praying it went unheard.

"I know, but it's obvious he's only doing it out of obligation since the Pillsbury Doughgirl can't get a real date."

My eyes squeeze tighter against her words, words I'd been running from my entire life, and as the room is filled with the sound of their laughter, I feel the pervasive sting of tears overwhelm me.

The girls find what they were looking for and leave as suddenly as they arrived. Renee places a comforting hand on my shoulder and squeezes reassuringly.

"They're bitches, Lay. Jealous bitches. They're not worth wasting your time on."

I give her a shaky smile. *"I know, but they have a point. He's only taking me to prom because I told him I wasn't going to go, and he insisted I had to."* I screw up my face at the memory. "It's really not fair. He deserves to go with a girl he likes and have the entire experience."

Renee scoffs. "We both know Ethan doesn't do anything he doesn't want to. He's taking you because he wants to."

"I don't know." My voice is quiet and unsure. Ethan has an overdeveloped sense of obligation, always determined to do the right thing. The last thing I ever want to be to him is a burden.

"Maybe I'll just tell him I got a date, that way he can go with whoever he wants to." I move away from the sink and place my brushes into their jars. Renee follows, and I can hear her muttering under her breath.

"What?"

"I said, you're killing me. But if you're determined to do that, I might be able to help."

"How?"

"You know my friend Luke? He moved here a few months ago from Ohio. Well, his girlfriend was going to fly down for prom, but she had to back out because her dad lost his job, so now he's going solo. He's a good guy, I'm sure he'd be happy to take you."

As we gather up our bags, I consider her suggestion and with Jasmine's voice ringing in my ears, I turn to her sadly.

"I'm in, set it up.

CHAPTER TWENTY-TWO

ETHAN

*T*urning off the shower, I step out of the stall and wrap a towel around my waist. The locker room is eerily quiet. Training finished over an hour ago, but while everyone else showered and left, I sat down with the coaches and had a long overdue discussion about my commitment to the team. Or lack of commitment.

It was a difficult conversation, but we all agreed it was in everyone's best interest for me to quit, and now that it's over, all I feel is relief. Now, I just need to sort out this shit with Layla and life will be good again.

I move through into the locker room, leaving the steam of the showers behind me and try to come up with a game plan for tomorrow. Layla's refused to see me all week, but we have our art history class tomorrow afternoon and I need to figure out my approach, so I don't spook her.

I'm lost in my thoughts, reaching up to open my

locker, when the door to the room is thrown open and Layla stands there, breathing heavily.

"There you are!" she screeches, pointing at me. "I've been looking for you everywhere!"

She's completely blindsided me and I stand there stunned as my eyes eat her up. Suddenly, she's moving toward me and throws herself in my arms, wrapping her legs around my waist and clashing her mouth with mine.

It takes a moment for me to wrap my head around what is happening, but as soon as I feel her pussy rubbing against my hardening cock my body acts on instinct.

I wrap an arm around her waist, holding her tight to my body, and my other hand threads through her hair, tugging it harder than I had intended. She pulls back slightly and starts trailing kisses along my neck, chanting something over and over, but her voice is a muffled whisper and I can't make out what she's saying.

Turning, I push her up against the lockers, pinning her with my hips, and I use both hands to cradle her face, searching her eyes in an attempt to figure out what's going on inside that head of hers.

Her face and neck are beautifully flushed, in a way that invites my mouth to taste her. To savor her.

"I love you."

My eyes snap to hers, her breathless confession stunning me.

"What?"

"I love you. I love you, and I know you messed up,

but I forgive you for that because I love you, and you love me. You spent fourteen years protecting me and loving me, and I couldn't see that, I *should* have seen that, but I didn't, and I know you left, but you never lied. Not ever, not once, so I believe you when you say you won't do it again." The words tumble out of her mouth, as though it can't keep up with her brain and her chest heaves, drawing my eyes to her chest. Her spectacular chest.

"Eyes up here, big boy." She tilts my head up and away from her tits. "I tell you I love you and all you can do is stare at my boobs?"

"They're impressive tits."

"Ugh, way to ruin the mood."

She stretches up and her mouth meets mine, her tongue sneaking out and aggressively thrusting in. Her nails scratch along my back and my hips jerk up involuntarily in response.

She breaks the kiss and unwraps her legs from my waist, planting her feet on the floor. My towel, which had come loose during our exchange and was only being held up by our bodies pressed together, falls to the ground and her eyes widen slightly at the sight of my cock standing straight up, straining toward her. It's been a long week, and my hand is no match for her warm, wet, pussy, so it's safe to say he's happy to see her.

She bites down on her bottom lip and if it was anyone else, that move would look calculating, but on her, it just looks sexy as fuck. My hands reach out to her, but she stops me. Using her own hands to press against my chest, she pushes me until the cold metal of the lockers is hard up against my back.

"What are you doing, Bug?"

She takes a step closer to me and I have to grab my dick and give it a tight squeeze to stop myself from coming from the look in her eye alone.

She slowly sinks to her knees in front of me, reaching over and placing my discarded towel under them. As though realizing where she is, she lifts her head and looks around the brightly lit room before looking at me from under her lashes.

"Don't look at me, okay? Just close your eyes or something."

My hands land in her hair and I make sure she holds my gaze. "Baby, if your mouth is going to be wrapped around my cock, I'm going to be watching."

I can see the battle raging across her face, the struggle of what she wants versus her embarrassment at being on display.

"I love you, Layla. You're beautiful and I want nothing more than your mouth on me, but if you don't want to, then that's okay too."

I mean every word I say, but my dick twitches angrily against my stomach, and I have a feeling he may never forgive me if he doesn't get inside her mouth soon.

She holds my stare for a moment and then with an almost imperceptible nod, she leans forward until her mouth is barely an inch from my crown, and in a move that will be forever burnt into my memory, her tongue pokes out and swipes along the slit. Her eyes close and a soft sigh escapes as the precum hits her tongue. The pornographic visual has my head falling backward, noisily, against the lockers.

"Are you okay?"

"I am so much better than okay." I grin down at her. "Don't stop on my account."

She licks her full, pink lips, and without further ado wraps her mouth around the head of my cock, sucking lightly while her hand comes up to hold my shaft, jerking cautiously.

I reach down and cover her hand with my own, squeezing it tight on every downstroke.

"Harder, Lay, you don't need to be so gentle."

She peeks up at me and nods, her mouth still full of my cock and I groan loudly at the sight.

I remove my hand and she continues the firm strokes while slowly taking more of me in her mouth. It doesn't take long before she grows more confident and her head bobs over my cock, coating it in saliva, and her tongue starts to tease along that sensitive spot at the base of my head. She finds her rhythm, her mouth and hand working in tandem, and when I look down to see her other hand slipping inside her leggings, and I feel her moan vibrate along my dick, the pressure becomes too much, and I rasp out a warning that I'm about to come.

She hollows out her cheeks and sucks even harder. My hands tighten in her hair, and I hold her immobile while the orgasm bursts through me, so fucking intense my knees almost give out.

When my vision returns to normal, I glance down

and see her looking up at me, her eyes a watery mess, and I notice her hands grasping my thighs, nails digging in. Quickly pulling back, my dick pops out of her mouth and she sucks in a deep breath, wiping her chin.

I instantly regret getting so carried away, and I tug her up to her feet, pulling her into me. "Are you okay?" I shake my head. "I didn't mean to... that was just..." I trail off, no idea how to finish that sentence.

She smirks up at me, her expression a far cry from the insecure-plagued one I faced twenty minutes ago.

"I'm good."

"Yeah, you fucking are." I laugh. "I swear to God, I don't ever want to know where you learned to do that, but I'll be forever grateful."

"Aw, Millhouse, I learned how to do that the same way every good girl does." She waggles her eyebrows at me. "Thank God for Cosmo!"

<hr />

Me: You having fun?

Layla: I'm trying to, stop bothering me!

Me: Can I come by your room tonight?

Layla: Evie will be there.

. . .

Me: No dirty business, just to sleep, I promise.

Layla: Yeah, okay. I'll let you know when I'm home.

Me: Good. I love you.

Layla: Love you too xox <3

I smile stupidly while reading her messages. The last few weeks have been pretty damn incredible, and I'm almost grateful to Cassidy for forcing Layla to figure her shit out. Because as good as I thought things were before Thanksgiving, now that she's finally all in, it's so much better.

"Get off your phone, you pussy-whipped mofo." Seth shoulders me out of the way. "It's your shot."

I pick up the pool cue and walk around the table, trying to pick my next shot. "Did Mia tell you where they were going?"

"No." He huffs. "She said if she told me, I'd turn up and crash their girls' night." I raise a knowing eyebrow. "Yeah, okay," he mutters.

"Guess I'm not the only pussy-whipped mofo, huh?"

"Shut up and take your shot, man." I laugh at his pissy expression, but I can't deny I'm right there with him. The girls decided they needed a night out before we all head home for the Christmas break, and no amount of arguing could convince them otherwise.

We finish our game and are just about to call it a night when a few of the guys from the football team turn up and convince us to stay for a few more drinks.

An hour and three beers later, the guys erupt in loud cheers when a group of girls walk in. My eyes immediately run over the crowd, searching for Layla and I'm disappointed when I don't find her. I check my phone to see if she's home yet, but when I come up empty, pocket it and return my attention to my friends.

"Well, hello boys." My lip curls up at the sound of Tash's voice and when she appears in front of us, her hands full of shots, I do my best to disguise my antipathy.

"Shot time, guys. Drink up, there's plenty more where they come from." She places them on the table in front of us and winks. While my friends whoop it up and down their drinks, I watch as she walks away, an exaggerated sway to her less-than-ample ass.

With a shake of my head, I lift the glass to my lips and swallow the shot in one gulp, grimacing against the burn.

I look up just in time to see Tash eyeing me with a sly look, so in an effort to ignore her, I grab another shot from the table in front of us. Throwing it back, I replace the glass upside down, and join the cries of "Shots!" echoing around the room.

CHAPTER TWENTY-THREE

LAYLA

"I can't believe I let you talk me into that." Evie rolls her neck, grimacing.

I choke on a laugh as I suck down water from my bottle. "You'll thank me for it later, I promise."

"You said that two hours ago," she groans.

"C'mon, let's go grab some breakfast, some greasy bacon will make you feel better." I take hold of her hand and tug her toward the I I know is only a couple of doors down from the gym.

The streets are unusually empty this morning. I guess everyone is recovering from their Friday night the same way Evie wishes she was – in bed, fast asleep.

Pushing our way into the small, cozy I, we're slapped in the face with the delicious aroma of sizzling bacon and brewing coffee and Evie groans orgasmically behind me.

While the streets outside were empty, inside, the almost-full bistro is filled with the warm hum of conversation. Grabbing one of the last available tables, we sink into the comfy padded chairs and Evie removes the sunglasses covering her tired eyes and glares at me.

"You know, I have no idea how you're sitting there all perky and awake, talking me into yoga at fuck o'clock in the morning." She shakes her head in frustration. "Why are you not hungover like the rest of us?"

"Because I didn't drink as much as the rest of you," I exclaim. Waving my index finger at her, I continue. "This is all self-inflicted, you're not getting any sympathy from me."

The waitress chooses that moment to take our order, halting Evie's protestations before they can even begin.

"So, talking about self-inflicted pain, did you ever hear anything else from Ethan last night?"

"Oh my God, no." I laugh. "He could barely get a sentence out when I called him, I think the guys ended up having a *huge* night. I'm sure he's home sleeping it off, and to be honest I don't really want to be around his hungover butt until he's feeling better."

"Hmph, I don't blame you, boys are the biggest babies," she scoffs.

Our food arrives, and we spend the next hour lazily enjoying our meal and chatting about pointless, irrelevant things. When Evie excuses herself to use the bathroom, I pull out my phone and can't hide my disappointment when there is no message notification. Consoling myself with the knowledge that Ethan will call when he's up, I decide to check my social media and log onto my Instagram account.

My mouth drops in horror as I scroll through my feed and see the same picture reposted over and over, the hashtags #whosbeenabadboy #weseeyou and #naughtynaughty swimming in front of my eyes.

My finger flies over the screen, and my mind shuts down in self-preservation when I realize what account posted the original picture: *@MillhouseMiller*.

The conversation I overheard in the library comes rushing back and I instinctively shake my head in denial. He hates Tash. *Hates her*. And he would never do this to me. *Never*.

But as every one of my insecurities screams in my ear, I realize his undeniable betrayal is staring me in the face. In vibrant tecnicolor.

"Hey, you wanna see a movie later? That new Mila Kunis one looks funny." I hear Evie approach me from behind, but my mind is too sluggish to react.

"Oh my God, what the actual fuck? Why are Ethan and Tash in bed together?" she screeches. "Wait, are they naked?!"

I storm into our dorm room and silently start throwing clothes into a bag. Evie follows behind me, but while I am processing everything internally, she is raging.

"I'm going to kill the fucker." She holds up my laptop. "You want to take this?" I shake my head, wanting to eliminate as many points of contact as possible. "Okay, when will the Uber be here?"

I check my phone. "It's here." I toss a handful of

underwear into my bag and follow it with my phone, watching as it sinks to the bottom under a pile of cotton.

We race down to the parking lot and when I spot the car waiting for me, I start to head in that direction. Evie grabs my arm, stopping me and pulling me into her, wrapping me in a giant hug.

"Call me when you get home, okay? I know you're in shock right now, Lay, but I need you to hear me. You *need* to stay in touch and let me know how you are going." She loosens her grip and pulls back. "I don't know what the fuck happened, but there has to be an explanation." Her brow furrows in confusion. "This just doesn't make any sense."

As much as I want to agree with her, it's hard to argue with photographic evidence.

Ethan

I'm dying. I have to be dying, that can be the only reason my brain hurts so much. Flashes of last night start to come back to me. Shots. So many fucking shots. If I survive this, I swear to God I will never touch a drop of tequila again.

I feel movement from the other side of the bed, and I delight in the knowledge that even pissed out of my mind I still managed to get Layla in bed with me. Ignoring the hammering in my head, I try to motivate myself to roll over, so I can get my hands on her when suddenly the banging is no longer coming from my head, but from the door to my bedroom.

I groan loudly, my mouth trying to call out, begging whoever it is to stop, but my mouth feels like it's full of cotton wool and I can't seem to wrap it around any words.

"Ethan! Get your ass out here you motherfucking asshole and bring the skank with you. I'm going to kill you both!"

Mia's voice penetrates my skull painfully, but it's her reference to Layla as a skank that has me taking notice.

"What the fuck, Mia?" I croak out. I attempt to sit up, ignoring the pain when the urgency in Mia's voice sinks in.

My hand reaches out to rest on Layla's hip, but when it lands on a curve that is decidedly *not* Layla's, I'm suddenly wide awake and painfully sober.

"Mmmm." The faux sleepy moan draws my attention to the face of the girl next to me, and my balls practically shrivel in horror when I realize it's Tash lying beside me.

Oh, fuck. My balls. I'm naked. And she's naked. This is so fucking bad.

"What the fuck, Tash?" I jump up off the bed and roar at her. "What are you doing here?" I look around my room, quickly spotting my boxers and throwing them on.

The hammering on the door starts up again. "Ethan! Out here, now!"

Tash grimaces humorously.

"Eeek."

Yep, she actually *said*, eek. "It doesn't sound like your friend is too happy about your upgrade, babe."

"What are you fucking doing in my bed, you crazy bitch?"

She sits up, holding the sheet to her chest and looks at me like a wide-eyed innocent. "Well, that's just mean. You were desperate to get me in your bed last night, and now you're calling me names?"

I shake my head manically. There's no way in hell, drunk or not, that I would ever want her in my bed.

"Ethan!"

I storm over to my door and yank it open. "What?!" I yell.

I never see the slap coming, but the sting of her hand certainly leaves its mark.

"Asshole!"

I step back, stunned at her aggression and look up to see Seth watching this shitshow with a somber expression on his face.

"And you!" She stalks toward Tash, pointing at her angrily. "Get your ratchet ass out of that bed, throw your skanky clothes back on and fuck off!"

Tash looks stunned, turning her head between the two of us. I guess she's looking to me for some backup, reassurance that she can stay. But there's no way in hell she's getting it.

"You need to leave."

Her eyes narrow bitterly at the sound of my calm voice.

"You're an asshole, Ethan." Mia throws her clothes and Tash starts dressing under the sheet.

"I'm not the asshole in this situation. I don't know what pathetic game you think you're playing, but if you tell anyone about this, I'll make sure everyone knows exactly how desperate you are."

Standing up, she grabs her shoes and purse from the floor, smirking at me. "It might be a bit late for that, baby." And she struts out, as though this is an everyday occurrence for her.

I scrub a hand over my face, relieved that she's gone. Deciding coffee can only make this morning better, I turn to head for the kitchen and come face to face with Mia staring at me incredulously.

"What? I didn't touch her, Mia, so you can wipe that look off your face. Even if I had wanted to – which I *didn't* – I was too wasted to do anything. This is just some bullshit kind of crazy that Tash is trying to pull."

"You need to see this." Seth's voice is abnormally serious, and he thrusts his phone in my face.

"Fuuuuck." My heart drops as I see picture after picture of Tash and myself, naked, on his Instagram feed.

"Who the fuck posted that?" My voice is hard, the need to lash out filling me violently.

"Who posted it?" Mia shrieks. "You fucking did!"

My feet pound along the hallway and I almost fall on my ass as I come to a stop in front of Layla's door. I thump on the door and pray she hasn't seen the picture yet. I have a much better chance of explaining myself if she doesn't have that visual in her head.

I bang on the door again and I notice a girl I don't recognize come strolling up the corridor toward me. When she gets close enough, I notice the squint of her eyes, the straight line of her mouth and as she passes by behind me, I hear the quiet whispered, "Asshole."

Shit. I raise my arm to knock on the door again when it's suddenly yanked open and a very pissed off Evie is standing there.

"Where is she?" I demand.

"As if I would tell you." Her voice matches mine in determination.

"Layla!" I try to stick my head in the room and get in far enough to see she's not there. "Where is she, Evie?"

"She's not here." Her hands land on my chest and she pushes with her entire weight. "And now, we need to make it so that you're not here either."

"I didn't fuck Tash." My voice breaks in anguish, not underestimating how important it is that she believes me.

"Well, it sure looked like it. I'm *so* pissed at you, Ethan." She clenches her teeth and closes her eyes. "I encouraged her to be with you. I was Team Fucking Ethan, and you do *this* to her?"

"I didn't do anything, you need to believe me. I don't know what bullshit game Tash is playing, but I didn't touch her."

She stands back, still blocking the doorway. "You

know you didn't touch her, or you *hope* you didn't touch her? Because Layla said you were pretty drunk when she spoke to you."

I rub my palm over my forehead, my earlier headache back with a vengeance. I know I was wasted last night, but I also know without a shadow of a doubt I would never risk my relationship with Layla, no matter how off my face I was.

"I *didn't* touch her. Where is she, Evie? I need to talk to her."

"I promised I wouldn't tell you." She at least has the decency to look apologetic. "She needs some time to think."

"We both know that's not what she's going to do." I shake my head bitterly. "She's going to turn inside herself and invent some narrative that fits her insecurity and gives her an excuse to walk away."

"Well, I guess you better figure out a way to stop that from happening. And you better do it quickly."

CHAPTER TWENTY-FOUR

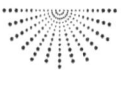

LAYLA

"*O*kay, so I've done some sketches to go along with the story you emailed me." Wyatt smiles at me. "It's such a cute story, by the way, I think you're going to ace this assignment."

I force a smile. "Thanks." I look through the pile of drawings she's handed me, and my smile becomes genuine. "These are amazing, Wyatt. I can't thank you enough for helping me out."

"I was happy to do it, it was a challenge, but I had fun."

I move around her studio apartment, my eyes flitting around restlessly. The tiny space is overflowing with furniture and art equipment, but rather than feeling cramped, it has a cozy, lived-in feel.

"Have a seat, sweetheart, I'll make us some tea and we can talk about the assignment a bit more."

I nod indifferently and settle on her little loveseat while she moves around the small kitchen. She has the radio playing softly in the background and my heart stutters slightly when I hear the lyrics playing.

I walked away, broken,
    Shattered by my own hand,
    Chasing my demons,
    I never stood a chance.

I crave the scent of her,
    Feel it linger on my skin,
    But that's just the fantasy,
    I'll never hold her again.

Wyatt carries our tea over, abruptly shutting the music off, and I sigh in relief.

"I swear that song is everywhere I go." I practically swoon "I forget his name, but that guy is incredibly talented."

"Flynn Maguire," she answers robotically.

"Yeah, that's it. But that song is so freaking sad, it has me in tears every time I hear it."

Wyatt smiles sadly. "I know the feeling." She reaches over and gives my hand a squeeze. "So, how are you doing?"

"I guess you've heard about what happened?"

"I did. Cassidy and Skye are worried about you. I hate to say it, and please don't hold it against me," she flashes me a worried look. "But, it's kind of nice to see Cassidy thinking about something other than Mason."

"Ugh, I know. I feel so bad for our parents, it was not a happy Christmas this year, with both of their daughters miserable." I bite my lip, thoughtfully. "Do you think CJ will work it out with him? I really thought they were good together."

"I don't know." She shrugs. "If you'd asked me two months ago, I would have said yes, but I'm afraid they've missed their chance now."

"You think people only have a certain window of time to fix a relationship?"

She considers me earnestly. "I know you want me to say no, and I wish I could, but I believe there is. Once it closes, it's too painful to put your pride aside and risk the rejection. Nobody wants to experience that kind of pain more than once. It's human nature to do whatever you can to protect yourself."

I feel the familiar sting in my nose, followed by the burn of my eyes.

"I'm sorry, I didn't mean to upset you. I'm probably not the best person to ask for love advice." She shifts uncomfortably in her chair and I regret asking the question.

"It's okay, I appreciate your honesty."

"Have you talked to him yet?"

The past two weeks play through my mind. Ethan blew up my phone the first couple of days, but I ignored his messages and voicemails. In fact, I've still yet to read or listen to them. He figured out pretty quickly that I was home and he turned up daily despite being turned away by my mother. His last visit was on Christmas day and my mom pulled out the big guns, sending my father out to deal with him. I have no idea what he said, but I haven't seen or heard from Ethan since.

"No, I just don't know what he could say. I mean, I saw the photo, and I want to believe that it's not what it looks like. I've tried to consider it from every angle, consider every explanation for it, and the only one that makes any sense is that he cheated on me." My hands tighten around my mug and I shake my head because there's a part of me that still can't believe he would do this to me. "And even if he didn't actually sleep with her, which, really, considering they were both naked is hard to believe, I'm still not okay with my boyfriend being in bed naked with another girl."

Wyatt doesn't say anything for a moment, she keeps her gaze locked on the window contemplatively. Suddenly turning toward me, she reaches down and places her tea on the small table in front of the loveseat.

"Okay, I can't tell you what to do, Lay. Every relationship is different, every *situation* is different, but I will say this." Inhaling deeply, she appears to be steeling herself for something.

"I was in a relationship a long time ago. We were going through some things and he left. He just ran away, no explanation, no chance for me to explain anything, he was just gone." Her voice thickens, and she chokes out the last word. I instinctively reach for her, but she waves me off.

"I know you don't want to hear this, but you owe it to yourself, and to him, to hear him out. If you can't live with his explanation, so be it."

I watch as she chews on the inside of her cheek, swallowing hard. "But living with the unknown will eat you up and you'll never be able to move on."

Ethan

"What can I get you?"

"An explanation would be a start, April."

The petite brunette's eyes fly to mine and her pen hovers over her pad, frozen in shock.

"Uh, h-hi Ethan, did you want to order?"

"No, I want you to sit down and talk to me."

"I can't, I'm working." Her voice is unsteady.

I look around the almost-empty diner and shake my head. "I'm sure you can take a break. You owe me this, April. You *owe* me."

She closes her eyes and gnaws on her bottom lip. "Okay, just give me a minute."

I watch her walk away and try to keep a hold on my temper.

After Layla refused to see me, I knew I had to get to the bottom of what had happened that night. I needed to have more than just my gut feeling to prove to her that I would never cheat.

It only took a few questions, and twenty bucks to the bartender, to learn that Tash and her friend, April, had been responsible for the steady stream of shots sent to us. And it was a very sober Tash and April who dragged my drunk ass out of there when everyone else was too wasted to notice.

April slides her ass onto the seat opposite me, all false bravado, and bites out an annoyed, "What do you want?"

"You need to tell me what happened that night."

"I don't know what you're talking about." She plays with a sugar packet nervously and I see right through her.

"Bullshit," I snap. "I already know you and Tash left the bar with me, and I know there's no way in hell I touched that bitch, so tell me what the fuck happened." I slam my hand on the table and she jumps at the sound.

"Ugh, Jesus, relax will you. It's not a big deal."

"Not a big deal?" I yell, ignoring the looks my outburst attracts. "My girlfriend thinks I cheated on her. She won't even talk to me."

"Well, it's not much of a relationship then, is it? If she doesn't trust you." She rolls her fucking eyes at me.

"Are you fucking kidding me right now?"

"Listen, Ethan, I don't know what to tell you. Tash wants you, and when she realized you fucked her and chucked her during your last break from the queen of the nerds, she decided you deserved a bit of payback." She glares at me across the table. "You really hurt her, you know."

"Wait, what?" My hand kneads the back of my neck in confusion. "I never slept with Tash. I've never dated her, never fucked her and definitely never given her indication that I ever would."

April watches me intently, and I can see her trying to gauge how truthful I'm being.

"Look, April, it sounds like she's played you, too. I promise you, I never laid a hand on her and I never did anything to make her think I would. I love my girl-friend and I would never do anything to mess that up." I lay my hands flat on the table in front of me, trying to calm myself.

April's fingers worry the sugar packet between her fingers even harder and she stares out across the restaurant.

"Tash said you were telling her you wanted her, but that you felt guilty dumping Layla. She said when you broke up—"

"We never broke up," I interrupt.

"Whatever. She said you did and that you slept with her and told her you wanted to be with her. Then when Layla came running back, you dropped her, but offered to keep screwing her on the side."

My face creases in horror at the idea. "That's complete bullshit."

She shrugs disinterestedly. "I guess. She was pretty convincing."

"So, what happened that night?"

"Christ, nothing, okay? Nothing happened! We took you home, stripped you off and Tash got into bed with you. I used your phone to take the photos, we posted it on your Instagram and I went home."

My head is about to explode at the vindictiveness of

the whole situation. How could someone be prepared to disrupt a person's entire life out of fucking *jealousy*. Holding onto my temper, I ask the most important question. The reason I'm here in the first place.

"Will you repeat this to Layla?"

Layla

I pace the floor of my dorm room, completely agitated as I consider what I'm going to do. After my talk with Wyatt, I realized I need to talk to Ethan. Good or bad, I need to know what happened, so I can move on. Maybe without him, but I can't deny I'm hoping it's with him.

I spent so many years pretending my feelings didn't exist, and in one moment of despair I had unintentionally taken this huge, life-altering leap. I risked a friendship that meant the world to me to take a chance on a love that meant everything. And I can't bring myself to regret it, because that moment had shifted the axis of my world and afterward everything had felt right, in a way it never had before.

Tired of being cooped up in this tiny room, I grab my jacket and decide to run to the dining hall for a late dinner. The air is freezing, and I pull my jacket tighter around me in an effort to ward off the cold. Thankfully, it's only a matter of minutes before I burst into the warm hall and I look around, rubbing my hands over my cheeks to warm them up, grateful it's so quiet.

After doing a quick scout, I grab some comfort food; fried chicken and mac and cheese, and take a seat in the farthest corner where, hopefully, I'll go unnoticed.

I pull my Kindle out of my purse and get lost in a fantasy world where everyone gets their own happily-ever-after while I eat my meal, blissfully oblivious to the world around me. Until the sound of a chair scraping along the floor drags me back to reality.

I glance up to see the last face I expected, sitting across from me.

"Tash."

You would think I would be angry. Ready to scream and cuss at the friend who possibly betrayed me just as significantly as my boyfriend. Instead, all I feel is curiosity as she stares back at me, a glint of triumph in her eye.

"I hope you don't mind, but I saw you and I figured we should clear the air sooner rather than later."

"Clear the air?"

Her brow crinkles and I think I detect a flicker of annoyance at my calm expression.

"Look, Layla, you have nothing to be ashamed of. No one can blame you for wanting him. He's hot as fuck, and his father's football royalty. Every girl wants him. But, you have to admit, you're not really a good match for him."

"And you are, I suppose?"

She scrunches her nose up sympathetically. "We're so much better suited for each other, you have to see that. And we tried so hard to control ourselves, out of loyalty for you, but we just couldn't do it anymore. I'm sorry."

"You're sorry?" I ask in disbelief.

"*So* sorry, babe. We never wanted you to find out like that!"

Her words touch a nerve and I find myself considering, stupidly for the first time, how the photo was taken.

"Who took the photo?"

"Wh-what?"

"Who took the photo?" I repeat. "It's an easy question, Tash."

"I don't know, a bunch of us went back to his apartment. I guess one of them thought it would be funny to use his phone and take a picture." She stumbles over her words. "It doesn't really matter, does it? The photo was taken and now you know." She eyes me kindly. "I think it's best if we just move on now. Ethan and I are together, and the gossip will die down a hell of a lot quicker if you just accept it. I know the last thing you want is to be the subject of gossip. You'd hate that."

She's right, I would. But something about her explanation isn't sitting right. Ethan never invites groups of people back to his place. He only tolerates large groups for small periods of time and would never put himself in a situation where he can't make a quick escape.

I gather up my trash, ready to leave. "Well, thanks for giving me your side of things, I appreciate it. I think I still need to talk to Ethan though."

"No!" she snaps. "Jesus, Layla, get a fucking clue. You talk to him and you're just going to force him to lie to you."

Ethan doesn't lie.

"You don't want me to talk to him?"

"It's not that I don't *want* you to." Her voice is teeming with aggravation. "It just won't achieve anything."

Standing up, I nod in agreeance. "Right."

"So, you won't say anything to him?"

I consider how to best answer her as I throw my purse over my shoulder, and in the end, decide the best response is no response.

"Take care, Tash."

❦

I spend the walk back to my dorm pressing the redial button on my phone, the need to talk to Ethan overwhelming me with a desperation I haven't felt since the moment I laid eyes on that horrific picture.

I enter the dorm and make my way up to my room on the verge of tears, grateful that Evie isn't back from break yet, and I can indulge in hours of self-pity with no judgment.

Turning the corner, I stop in shock when I see Ethan sitting on the floor next to my door, his head in his hands. I take a step forward and the tears that have been threatening, finally spill. I bite down on my lip, hard, in an attempt to stop them, but I fail.

I must make a noise because Ethan's head turns in my direction and a look of relief filters over his face. He rises slowly, and I notice how tired he looks. I'm filled with remorse, wishing we'd had this conversation weeks ago.

"I heard you were back." He remains standing where he is, his hands shoved in his pockets and he looks more unsure than I've ever seen him before.

I pull my sleeve down and scrub my face before moving toward him, submitting to the need to be close to him.

When we're face to face, my breathing becomes shallow and I notice he removes his hands and his fists clench, as though he's trying to keep his hands off me.

"Hi."

I huff out a small laugh. "Hey."

"She set me up, Bug. I didn't sleep with her, I swear to God, I didn't." His voice is pained, and I want to relieve that pain intensely.

"I know." His eyes widen in surprise and I smile, trying to reassure him.

"Let's go inside." I push past him and open the door to my room, dropping my purse on the desk. "Do you want a drink?"

He shakes his head, looking at me as though I'm crazy. "No, I want to know what you mean by 'I know.'"

I grab a bottle of water, purely so I have something to occupy my hands. "I just saw Tash in the dining hall."

"And she admitted what she did?" His voice rings with disbelief.

"No, but she told me not to talk to you or you would lie to me."

He leans back against the desk, his shoulders slumping. "I don't get it, why would that convince you I didn't fuck her?"

I squeeze my eyes shut against his crass words, and sigh. "Because you don't lie, Ethan. You've never lied to me. I believe that if you wanted to be with someone else, you'd tell me. But you know who does lie?" I pause briefly, but not long enough for him to reply. "Tash lies. So, I had to decide what's more likely. You cheating on me and lying about it, or Tash somehow manipulating a situation to make me believe you cheated on me."

"And you believe me?" His voice catches in his throat.

"I believe you," I confirm.

He sits there nodding his head, not saying anything, just nodding like a loon, until a giant smile spreads over his face. He launches at me, tackling me to the bed and kissing me senseless.

I laugh against his mouth, feeling the stress of the past two-and-a-half weeks drain away.

"I love you." I pull away from him, just far enough that I can see his face. "I need to stop doubting you and I promise I'm going to try. But—" I squeeze his cheeks with one of my hands. "If I ever see a photo of you in bed, naked, with another woman, I will cut your penis off. Got it?"

He laughs wildly, his happiness evident. "Sounds like a fair deal."

His mouth finds mine again and we spend seconds,

minutes, hell, maybe even hours indulging in the intimate touches I've been craving. Our hands become more demanding, and as our bodies seek out the relief we've been missing, I make a promise to myself to never stop trusting that this man sees me when I can't see myself, and he's got me anytime I need to be caught.

EPILOGUE

ETHAN

 *ive Years Later*

"Look at this."

A magazine is thrust at my face and I snatch it away, glaring at Seth, before glancing at the cover.

"People? Really, Parker? Although, I guess it's a step up from the Enquirer."

"Just look, asshole."

Taking another glimpse, my eyes widen when I see the cover story. A scandalous cheating headline accompanies a variety of pictures of a pissed-off Michael Bradshaw, storming out of his house and abusing photographers, and a half-naked Tash Bradshaw, dancing on a nightclub table with a cocktail in each hand.

"Well, fuck me." I grin across at Seth. "I can't say I'm surprised, though."

"I can." I do a double take at his words, because, well, really? "Surprised it took this fucking long to come crashing down."

"I feel sorry for their kid, though. With parents like that, her life can't be easy."

"Tell me about it." Mia strolls into the large banquet hall where Seth and I are standing by the door, supervising the set-up for tonight's party. "Those two are like a what-not-to-do parenting guide, coming to you courtesy of every gossip magazine." She pauses, rubbing her small bump before looking around the room, appreciatively. "This place looks beautiful. Layla's going to love it."

I follow her gaze, taking it all in with a sense of pride. The room is decorated in various shades of pink, with elegant – so I'm told – touches of silver thrown in. Sheer white drapery lines the walls, backlit with muted pink lights that cast a romantic glow over the room, and the huge, hanging chandelier in the middle of the ceiling adds to that romanticism. Yeah, Bug is going to love it.

"Okay, Parker, your ass is mine now." Mia's voice snaps me out of my thoughts and I turn my attention back to them.

"I need to get you ready." She turns to me. "Are you going to be okay here?"

"Yeah, we're almost finished. Can you let Layla know I'll be up soon?"

She nods distractedly, her brows furrowed as she watches Seth, who is doing some weird little jig on the spot.

"What are you doing?" she finally shrieks in exasperation.

Seth stills, looking at Mia over his shoulder. "I'm practicing my dance moves."

I laugh at his bewildered expression while Mia just groans and pushes him toward the door. Before she can follow, I quickly grab her hand, stopping her.

"How's she doing?"

"She's fine, Ethan." Her eyes soften. "A bit nervous at the idea of being the center of attention, but more excited to see everyone." She places her hand on top of mine and squeezes, reassuringly. "She's going to be fine."

I give her a small smile and watch as she follows Seth out. I'm grateful they also got a room in the hotel where we're holding the party, it's been a lifesaver having Seth help me out while Mia kept Layla distracted.

I roam around the room, watching people race around putting on all the finishing touches until I find myself standing in front of the gift table. The wall behind it is covered with a beautiful photo display that Layla's friend Wyatt created.

The collage is a depiction of Layla's life and I'm struck by how many pictures feature the two of us together, a wave of gratitude for this woman washing over me.

My mind wanders to the magazine article I just saw. There's no doubt the karma train found Bradshaw and Tash, and a twinge of satisfaction rolls through me. Those two have been together since a one-night stand ended in a surprise pregnancy, not long after Layla and I got together. And since he got drafted into the NFL after graduation, they've been living a very public life of breakups and makeups.

In contrast, the past five years have been very kind to Layla and me, and we're building a life that, for so long, I never dreamed was possible.

We're both happy in our careers, me working my way up in the architecture firm where I did my internship in college, and her as Miss Jensen to a never-ending parade of first-graders. Our life is quiet, and some might consider it small in comparison to the NFL dream that could have been mine. But our life together is full of love and I have never once regretted the decision I made. Football is for Sundays, not for life.

Her scent hits me before I see her, the light floral scent that I will always associate with her tickles my nose, just before her arms wrap around me from behind.

Turning to face her, I pull her tight to me. "You're not supposed to be down here." I lean down and place a kiss on her nose.

"I missed you." She looks up at me from under her lashes and I feel a jolt rush through me. Her eyes still slay me every single time.

"What's that?" She peers around me, attempting to see the photo display but I block her view.

"It's nothing. C'mon, let's go get ready." I turn her toward the door, and slip my hand in hers, twining our fingers together.

She follows me silently, but I see her eyes taking in the room and the soft smile that finds a home on her lips. My hand tightens around hers, and I take a deep breath, trying to calm my nerves and praying that tonight goes the way I hope it will, and we have another significant moment to add to our life collage.

Layla

I wander through the room that's filled with everyone I love and take a moment to appreciate how lucky I am.

"Aunty Layla!" I look down just in time to see my three-year-old niece throw herself at me.

"Mack, hey, baby. What're you doing?" I pick her up, reveling in the feel of her chubby arms wrapped around me.

"I'm hiding from Mommy."

I laugh loudly at her honesty. "If I had a dollar for every time I've heard that, Mackenzie Bug, I would be a very rich lady."

"Ugh, there you are, you little gremlin." Cassidy appears from behind me and Mack squeals. "You need to come and eat something."

"No!" Her little blonde ringlets bounce as she shakes her head and I watch as the two of them, both as stubborn as the other, glare at each other.

"Fine, don't have any dinner. I guess that means you don't want any chocolate cake. Seb, Summer, and Poppy will be happy to hear that."

"No! I want chockly cake!" She reaches out her arms to CJ who takes her and places her on the ground.

"Go see Daddy and Uncle Ben and they'll make you a plate."

Mackenzie runs off and we watch her weave her way through the crowd, throwing herself at Mason just as enthusiastically as she did to me just moments ago.

"God, I love her," I exclaim.

"She's a nightmare," Cassidy counters.

"Well, of course she is, she takes after you."

"Ha-ha, smartass." She throws an arm around me. "You having fun, bub?"

"I am. I really am."

"Good, I have to admit I thought Ethan was crazy throwing you a big party like this, but I guess he knows you best these days."

I smile because she's right. No one knows me as well as Ethan. I'm not sure they ever did.

Cassidy starts rambling about the birthday cake she made for the party and I return to my people-watching, tuning her out when I realize I've already heard this story twice before.

I spot Seth over in the corner, entertaining Mia, Evie, Wyatt, and Skye, Skye's youngest daughter, Poppy, on her hip. On the other side of the room my brother-in-law, Mason, and Skye's husband, Ben, are wrangling the older kids, trying to get them to sit down long enough to eat; and sitting at a table by the buffet, deep in conversation are Ethan's and my parents.

I smile as I watch them all. It's a room full of love

and I sometimes still pinch myself at how lucky I am. Finally, my eyes search for Ethan. It's been awhile since I last saw him, and I have the need to feel his hands on me, no matter how briefly.

I turn to Cassidy, interrupting her. "Have you seen Ethan?"

Ethan

I watch her from the other side of the room. Watch her walk around this room filled with her friends and family and revel in the confidence she's exuding. Years and experience have seen her grow confidently into the person she was always meant to be. I like to think my love has helped, too.

But there are still moments, moments I wish she could see herself through my eyes. Or Evie's. Or, hell, the stranger on the street. I wish she could really see how beautiful she is. But I realize life doesn't work that way. All I can do is love her and make her feel secure in that love. The rest is up to her.

"You ready, man?" Seth slaps me on my shoulder.

"Yeah, good to go," I reply, sounding a lot more confident than I feel.

He motions to the DJ who cuts off the track he's playing and silences the crowd.

I step up onto the slightly raised platform the DJ has been performing on, nervously clutching the microphone in my hand.

"Hi everyone." I hold a hand up and wave. "I just want to thank everyone for coming tonight to celebrate Layla's birthday. I know it means a lot to her that you're all here, and it means a lot to me too." My eyes roam over the crowd, looking for the girl of the hour. "Speaking of the birthday girl, where is she?"

A cheer goes up toward the back of the room and I smile when I spot her, a huge grin on her face battling with the red flush of embarrassment.

"Lay, can you come up here?"

Her eyes narrow suspiciously, but with some gentle nudging from Cassidy, she makes her way to the front of the room until she's standing in front of me. Letting the microphone drop to my side, I step down and place a kiss on the corner of her mouth, letting my tongue sneak out for a quick taste.

"Hey, Bug."

"Hi," she whispers.

"Are you having fun?"

She's looking at me as though I'm insane. "What are you doing?"

I look up and I can see everyone's eyes locked on us curiously, wondering what's going on.

"I wanted to ask you a question."

"And you thought now was a good time?"

I chuckle at her disbelieving tone. "I think now is the perfect time. It's an important question and I wanted to have a lot of witnesses."

A wave of whispered excitement spreads through the crowd and I know the exact moment she realizes what is about to happen because her jaw drops and her eyes widen.

"Yes."

I laugh loudly at her excited shriek. "Yes?"

"Yes! Oh my God, yes!" She's wringing her hands, practically bouncing on the spot and I can't believe I get to spend the rest of my life with her.

"You kind of stole my thunder, Bug. Can I ask the question? I've been practicing for months."

"Oh, oh, I'm sorry, yes, ask! Ask the question!"

I kneel down in front of her and pull out the ring box I've been hiding for months. "Layla Rose Jensen, I've loved you since we were four, I've wanted you since we were twelve and I've needed you since I was twenty-one. Will you please marry me and let me love you, want you and need you, for the next sixty years?"

I see her lips form the word 'yes' rather than hear it, her whispered response drowned out by the whoops and cheers from our guests. But as the room erupts, I keep my attention zeroed in on her. The only woman I've ever wanted to see.

THE END.

I hope you enjoyed *Amongst the Wildflowers*! Keep reading for a sneak peek at book 4 in the *Finding Forever* series, ***Breathing Wisteria*** (Wyatt's story!), and please consider leaving a review.

***

Would you like a FREE book? Get your copy of Rule Breaker, a steamy student/teacher rom com HERE!

***

Also, don't miss the sneak peek of *Down the Rabbit Hole* by Joz Maxel at the end of this book, which is AVAILABLE NOW!

SNEAK PEEK: Breathing Wisteria by Amali Rose

PROLOGUE

WYATT

Ten Years Earlier

Smoke.

My nostrils twitch as the subtle acrid smell hits them and a sliver of unease curls itself around my consciousness.

The club is crowded, and I'm jostled carelessly between a sea of sweaty bodies. My hand instinctively finds my belly and I internally curse Flynn for convincing me to come tonight.

I crane my neck, searching for the source of the putrid smell, but I can barely see past the people surrounding me. Their clammy skin pressing against my own combined with their loud voices ringing in my ear, the atmosphere practically suffocates me.

My breathing begins to quicken. Short, shallow breaths that I have to fight to get into my lungs, heighten my anxiety and the mild apprehension I was feeling morphs quickly into full-blown dread that thrashes violently through my veins.

Closing my eyes, I try to block out the crowd around me and concentrate on Flynn's voice, which floats above the cheers and catcalls. My vision is blocked from my position over here, along the side of the room where I, wrongly, assumed I could avoid the crush of the congested dance floor.

That's when it happens.

With my eyes squeezed shut, one hand pressed against my hammering chest and the other curled protectively over my stomach. My brain shuts down, focusing only on the voice of the man I love, singing the song he wrote about us. About cherry Chapstick and cheap beer.

The moment my life was forever changed.

One word screamed.

Hundreds of bodies pushing, fighting each other, chased by the cruel heat and wicked burn.

I'm shoved forcefully up against the wall as people lose all sense of decency in their own fight for safety. My eyes flicker to my left and I see the orange flames dancing with the plumes of black smoke above the stage. My heart sinks and I unconsciously begin fighting against the crowd. Sweat prickles along every inch of my skin and I fight every instinct in me as I try to make my way toward Flynn.

A tall guy stops right in front of me, his face is panicked, and I can see a fear in his eyes that I know is echoed in my own. He bends down and grabs my shoulders, his fingertips digging in painfully. "Go the other way!" he screams in my face, his spit coating me. Shaking my head, I push past him and hear him mutter, "Stupid bitch."

The pungent smoke has filled the room and as my lungs struggle to cope, screaming for fresh air, I become disoriented. I spin around, my eyes burning while I attempt to gather my wits. But when a stray elbow connects with my already aching temple, I lose my balance, falling to the ground. And in a moment that I know will forever be imprinted on me, amidst the cacophony of terrified screams, flailing bodies, and heart-wrenching terror, I lose everything that I love.

CHAPTER ONE

WYATT

*T*his room is full of love. It's almost a tangible entity that I can physically feel and a small smile dances across my lips as I stand in a corner, taking it all in. My smile explodes into a loud laugh as I watch one of my best friends, Cassidy, chase her three-year-old twins around the room, a small plate of food in each hand and long cotton-candy-pink hair streaming behind her.

"I don't know how she handles those two." A gentle voice has me turning, and I see the last member of our trio, Skye, standing to my right, her own full mouth tilted in an amused smile.

"I struggle with my two, and Poppy is barely even walking. If I were getting double-teamed like that, I'd be waving the white flag." She groans.

I bring the champagne glass left over from our earlier toasts to my mouth and take a small sip, enjoying the way the bubbles tickle my throat on their way down.

"You know what?" My eyebrow quirks as I observe my beautifully ridiculous friend, who is the perfect, contradictory mix of virtue and venom, with her children. "If I ever doubted the existence of karma, that doubt vanished when she had Mack and Seb. I mean, look at that." I raise a finger from my glass and point toward Cassidy's parents on the opposite side of the room. They're watching the quiet chaos their grandchildren are causing, gleefully. "Cass' mom is practically giddy watching her chase those babies around. I'd say that's a pretty blatant example of karma biting you on the ass."

Skye snorts out an adorable laugh as she takes in the Jensens' expressions before she turns her attention to the newly engaged couple slow dancing in the middle of the room. The reason we're here celebrating tonight.

"So, how long do you think until those two start popping out some beautiful babies?" Skye tilts her head to Ethan and Layla, her warm blue eyes softening as we watch Ethan's grip on his new fiancée tighten and he pulls her even closer.

The pain that rips through my chest at her question is visceral and it takes everything I have to keep myself upright and a smile plastered on my face.

"My guess is we get an announcement in the next six months. I can't see them waiting," I reply, confidently.

Skye continues to watch them contemplatively, and I allow my mind to wander. My thoughts are trailing into dangerous territory when her next words take me completely by surprise and quickly snap me out of my dark reminiscences.

"I guess it's just you that we have to worry about now."

I whip my head around to face her, my eyes wide in surprise.

"What?"

She reaches across and takes the glass from my hand before gulping down the remains and placing the empty glass on a table beside her.

"Well, it's just you now. The rest of us are all married off, or as good as. Babies are popping out all over the place." She looks pointedly over to a large table where Cassidy has managed to wrangle Mackenzie and Sebastian, getting them seated alongside Skye's children, Summer and Poppy. Cassidy and her husband, Mason, are looking flustered as they deal with a pissed-off Mack (seriously, can you say, like mother, like daughter?) and Skye's husband, Ben, feeds Poppy and watches on indulgently while Seb sneaks his much-loved potato chips to his much-loved Summer.

"Now we just need to get you married off and we can all be horrible hot messes together!"

My face heats at her declaration and for the millionth time since I met these women all those years ago, I regret holding on to my secrets so fiercely.

"Yeah, that's not going to happen, sweetie, so don't hold your breath." I hate the steel tone my voice carries.

Skye's eyes narrow shrewdly as she watches me and I'm sure she must be able to hear my heart thrashing wildly in my chest. Unbidden, my hand flies to my breast, my palm attempting to soothe the pain away.

"One day you're going to tell me, you know."

The ache intensifies at her words and a flush of anxiety washes over me.

"Tell you what?" Denial. I'm an old hand at this particular method of self-preservation and the words slip out of my mouth with practiced ease.

Skye's hand finds mine and she gives me a gentle squeeze.

"When you're ready, I will be here for you. I need you to know that."

One thing you learn about Skye very quickly is that she may look like an angel, all innocent beauty and wide-eyed optimism, but she will have your back, no questions asked. Anytime, anywhere.

I clench my jaw and my teeth grind against each other. A lump solidifies in my throat making it impossible for me to do anything other than nod.

No matter how desperately I wish I could unburden my heart, it's impossible to change the past. I have no choice but to continue to keep these scars hidden because, honestly, I'm not sure they could ever forgive me for concealing such a huge piece of my heart from them.

As if this moment couldn't get any worse, the song that was the soundtrack to the worst year of my life starts playing over the sound system. A song declaring true love and the desire to save something worth fighting for. Memories immediately run through my mind as I relive it all. Long fingers scrawling words, madly trying to get down the thoughts, emotions, and fears before they disappeared forever.

Skye's reaction to the song is vastly different. Her face transforms when she hears the opening chords, the air between us immediately defusing, and her hand grips my wrist.

"Oh my God, I love this song! Can you watch the girls for a minute?" She gives me her best puppy dog eyes. "I want to dance with Ben."

Slipping on my best neutral mask, I agree and follow her back to our table.

"C'mon, babycakes, hand the mac and cheese to Wyatt and come and dance with me."

Ben grins beautifully at his wife, his eyes crinkling up in amusement, and my mask slips briefly as I let a moment of wistfulness overwhelm me.

Remembering, just for a brief moment, the way guarded brown eyes used to look at me as though I was perfection personified.

Until they didn't.

Shaking my head slightly, I reach over and take the small bowl from his hands and gesture for Ben to go. He leans over and places a swift kiss on my cheek, along with a whispered thank-you.

I can't stop my eyes from following them across the dance floor and just when I start to feel those old papered-over cracks in my heart start to split again, Cassidy's voice snaps me out of my reverie.

"Ugh, those two make me want to puke. No one should still be that lovey-dovey after all this time. That is not what marriage is."

Mason smirks across at her, running a hand through his tousled brown hair. "I don't know, we were pretty lovey-dovey this morning, if you recall."

She narrows her eyes at him, and I prepare myself for whatever scathing comment is to come. Looking at Mason, his grin has widened and he's practically vibrating with anticipation. I suppress an eye roll. I've never met a man who enjoys getting his balls busted so much by his wife.

But before she can say anything, a loud cry sounds when Mackenzie falls off her chair, crashing to the ground. Cassidy rushes to pick her up and is soothing her when Seb abruptly stands up on his chair, looking anxiously around the room. Mason tells him to sit down in a commanding voice that almost has my ass finding a seat, but Seb just looks at him, his eyes wide.

"I need to go to the potty, Daddy."

Mason moves quickly, reaching over to pick him up, but when his hand lands on Seb's butt a loud groan escapes.

"You didn't make it, huh, bud?"

Cassidy continues soothing Mackenzie, who is still loudly screaming and looks at her husband and son, both of whom are now covered in pee.

She turns to me slowly, a sardonic look on her face.

"This," she says calmly. "This is marriage."

❧

The bed dips beneath me and I flop back onto the mattress, arms spread, eyes closed.

Tonight was... I'm not even sure what it was.

Seeing my friends all together in one place, so happy with their partners and children, it created a huge mess of conflicting emotions.

And memories. So many painful memories.

Sheets rustle under me when I turn to my side and reach under the bed for the box. The box.

Where said memories are supposed to go and die a swift death.

But they don't. They merely hibernate in there until the next time my defenses are down, and I can't stop from torturing myself.

Sitting back up, I cross my legs and place the large box over my legs.

Five years. Inside this ridiculous-looking box covered in garish pink flamingos is five years of my life.

Four years of immeasurable joy. One year of immeasurable pain.

My throat tightens while my fingertips move, almost involuntarily, ghosting across the top and my heart thunders as I try to compose myself before facing my nightmare.

So, essentially, my usual reaction.

Taking a deep breath, I do my best to steady my hands and I slowly remove the lid. Lying on top is the framed photograph that sat on my bedside table for almost two years. I'm wearing a gorgeous pink dress with a long, ruffled skirt. If I close my eyes, I can still feel the soft material tickling my ankles.

I tripped over that damn thing so many times and

very nearly ended the night with a sprained ankle. Plus, it clashed wildly with my bright red hair, but I couldn't have cared less. I loved that dress so damn much and the boy staring down at me in the photograph seemed to agree.

Although, if I recall he was just as eager to get it off me as he was to admire it on.

I reach up and scrub a hand over my nose which is developing the unmistakable tingle of oncoming tears. Christ, I must be getting sappy in my old age, I normally last longer than this.

Sliding my eyes back to the photo, I take in the tall, built guy next to me, his intense brown eyes glued to me as I grin at the camera. Full lips that so rarely lifted into anything more than a dirty smirk, are curled up into a smile so big, it almost rivals my own.

He towers over me, and I remember the sense of safety that used to overwhelm me every time his arm slid around my shoulders and he would pull me in, close to his body. The sensation of his calloused fingers on my skin when they would inevitably start teasing along the curve of my neck.

He was my home. Wherever he was, that was where I was supposed to be.

Where I wanted to be.

Until I didn't.

Sighing, I shove the picture back into the box, aggressively.

Flynn. Fucking. Maguire.

One of the biggest singer-songwriters in the music

industry is my ex. My first love. The man I stupidly thought I would spend the rest of my life with.

Now, as the song says, he's just somebody I used to know. Somebody who is impossible to escape, no matter how hard I try. His face appears on my Facebook feed incessantly, in magazines, on television.

Don't even get me started on his music. It's everywhere. So many songs that he wrote when we were together, and I'm immediately propelled back in time, remembering the way his voice would deepen when he had an idea that he was passionate about. The way he would get so lost in creating he would forget to do simple things, like, you know, eat.

Biting down hard on my lip, I dive back in, sorting my way through piles of random snapshots, corny love notes and lyrics scrawled in his god-awful writing.

The pain of missing him is savage, intensifying as each memory washes over me, and only when I notice the wet heat on my face, do I realize that my tears have finally fallen.

I allow myself to feel this so rarely and this is exactly why. It's too much. Too much pain, too much regret.

Too much everything.

I begin to gently place everything back in the box when my eye catches on the corner a picture sticking out of an envelope. Suddenly I miss the pain of only moments before, because this agony right here? It is the soul-crushing, life-altering kind.

Pain that changes you into a person you no longer recognize.

Dropping everything in my hands, I pull the photo out of the yellowing envelope and lock onto the grainy black and white picture.

My chest heaves, my eyes burn, and my throat feels as though it's closing up as that tiny image reduces me to a violent vortex of grief.

Quickly stuffing the photo back into the box, I dump everything else on top of it and replace the lid, wishing desperately it was that easy to hide my pain away. I lean down and shove the evidence of my life gone so wrong under the bed, before giving in to the cleansing sobs that are fighting to escape.

Reaching over to my purse that is still lying on the bed, I pull out my cell phone and manage to calm myself so I'm only a snotty, hiccupping mess, rather than a snotty, sobbing one.

Unlocking my screen, I search through my contacts and pull up the name I should have called a long time ago.

With a shaking finger I press the call button, take a deep breath, and wait for the call to connect.

Breathing Wisteria is **AVAILABLE NOW!**

Stay Connected

Private Facebook Group: https://www.facebook.com/
groups/amalisrisqueromantics
BookBub: https://www.bookbub.com/
authors/amali-rose
Facebook: https://www.
facebook.com/authoramalirose
Goodreads: https://www.goodreads.com/author/
show/17064277.Amali_Rose
BookBinge: https://bookbinge.com/author/amali-rose
Instagram: https://www.
instagram.com/authoramalirose
TikTok: https://vm.tiktok.com/ZS3KAon3/

My newsletter is the best way to stay in contact with
me! You'll get first look at titles, covers and release
dates, plus exclusive sneak peeks!
Sign up here: https://tinyurl.com/y6h3hw9s

More by Amali Rose

Finding Forever Series
(Standalone series)

Under the Cherry Blossoms >> Fling to Forever
Romance
Dandelion Dreams >> Enemies to Lovers/Office
Romance
Amongst the Wildflowers >> Friends to Lovers
Romance
Breathing Wisteria >> Second Chance Romance
Finding Forever>> The Complete Series

Greetings From Avondale Series
(Standalone Series)

Mistletoe Mistake >> Brother's Best Friend/Holiday
Romance
Miss Independent >> Billionaire Romance

Standalones:

Dating the DILF >> Single Dad Romantic Comedy

ACKNOWLEDGMENTS

Firstly, to all the bloggers who have read, reviewed and/or promoted any of my books, thank you so very much. I'm incredibly aware how tirelessly you all work to promote authors and you do it all for the love of books. Please know, you are appreciated, you are valued, and we truly couldn't do what we do without you. THANK YOU!!!!

As always, a huge thank you goes to my alpha readers, Kim and Tanya, and my beta readers, Heather, Rachel, Renee, Robyn, Tamara and Tre. I am so grateful, to all of you, for your feedback, opinions, support and encouragement. Thank you for dropping everything, every time I sent you chapters, and thank you so damn much for loving Layla and Ethan as much as I do.

Special thanks to Ellie from My Brother's Editor, and Stacey and Petrina from Spell Bound. This book would not be what it is without you, and I mean that from the bottom of my heart. Thank you for being so wonderful to work with and for putting as much care into my book baby as much as you did.

A big thank you to Ben from Tall Story Designs for another beautiful cover. You're amazing!

On the business end, I want to express my extreme gratitude to Kylie and Jo from Give Me Books. You ladies are so professional and absolutely brilliant to work with!

Joz, Kim, Antonette, Harper, Stacey, Sienna and Laura, thank you for always making me laugh, always pushing me through and always reminding me how happy I am to have you.

Tanya, I'm so lucky to have you in my corner. Love your guts!

Rachel, thank you for helping me run the ST, and your constant and unwavering support. Forever my favourite Kiwi!

Kerry (and Ella!), Karen and Renee, I'm blessed to have you in my life and will never take your love and support for granted. Thanks for always being there.

My street team: Antonette, Cassy, Devon, Heather, Katrina, Kristi, Lauren, Rachel, Tamara & Tre. You girls are extraordinary. Thank you for believing in me as much as you do. I'm so lucky to have you!

To my readers. Thank you, thank you, THANK YOU! You've waited a long time for this book and I hope you agree that it was worth the wait. Thank you so much for wanting to read my stories. It blows my mind that there are any of you out there, and I will never stop appreciating you.

Finally, this book is incredibly close to my heart. Sometimes the feeling that you're not enough, that you don't measure up and you don't deserve to be loved can be overwhelming. Loving yourself is so much harder than loving another person. We judge ourselves much too harshly, always so quick to believe the judgement of others. Other people who are themselves struggling through their own stories. I hope each and every person who has ever battled this, is able to one day see the true beauty that only they bring into the world.

"You alone are enough."
Maya Angelou

Huge love and hugs
Amali xox

ABOUT THE AUTHOR

USA Today Bestselling author Amali Rose is a former blogger from Australia, who released her debut novella in 2017.

A self confessed bookworm, her love affair with the written word began as a child, with *The Magic Faraway Tree*. Her tastes have grown and evolved over the years and, after stumbling into the indie community a few years ago, she discovered her passion for romance with a side of smut.

When not reading or writing, Amali enjoys cheesy pop music, netflix marathons, and she believes strongly that pink, puppies and chocolate make the world a better place!

SNEAK PEEK: Down the Rabbit Hole by Joz Maxel

PROLOGUE

 $\mathcal{M}$ y mother loves to entertain; no reason is too insignificant. Tonight's barbeque is different, though. My little sister, Nala, and I are going to meet the man my mother has been dating for the last couple months. It must be pretty serious because not only are we meeting Larry for the first time, but also his son, who still remains nameless.

The back yard is starting to fill with pretentious couples who look like they have never stepped foot on grass, let alone been to a barbeque. Some faces look oddly familiar, but from where, I couldn't for the life of me tell you. I'm guessing these are Larry's people. The only other detail I have, other than he has a son, is that he's a CEO for some oil company.

The one person I'm excited, yet nervous to see, is Thomas. I've been crushing on him for the past month, and he gave me my first kiss two nights ago. It was sweet, but unexpected. I passed over an invite to him from my mom, who said she would love to meet the boy who makes her daughter "perky".

"I wanted to apologize for last night. I shouldn't have gotten touchy-feely with you."

I nibble on the inside of my cheek. "No, it's okay. I liked it."

He turns to look at me and smiles. "Yeah? I was worried you hated me."

I shake my head, trying to quell the blush I can feel staining my cheeks. "I could never hate you."

He nudges my shoulder. "Never say never."

I spot Thomas coming through the side gate, scanning the crowd for me as I put the dish of hors d'oeuvres on the table. By the time I'm done arranging the other dishes, Thomas grabs my wrist and pulls me into the house.

"Thomas, wait. What are you doing?"

"I just want to be alone with you for a minute."

He continues leading me to the staircase and down the stairs, to the basement. I try loosening the grip he has on me, but the more I try to pry his fingers off, the stronger his hold gets.

My brain is firing off warnings that this isn't a good situation to be in.

"Thomas, stop. You're scaring me."

My heel catches on the edge of a stair and I fall into

him, almost throwing him off, but he steadies himself before reaching the bottom.

It's an unfinished, open plan with exposed insulation and ductwork. A mattress sits on the cold cement floor in the corner directly in front of us, and a washer and dryer are situated a few feet to the left. The only closed-in space is a closet my mom built specially for all her pageant dresses.

"What's in there?" He points to the double white doors as he continues walking toward them.

"Can you let me go, now that you know where the basement is?"

He looks over his shoulder with an insidious smile. "The fun hasn't even started yet."

"I'll scream bloody murder if you don't let me go."

I claw at his arm, trying to get him to let go. With his free hand, he gets one of the doors open, pulls me inside and shuts the door. The lights flicker on, bathing us in a soft glow, as Thomas leans against the door, blocking my only way of escape.

I feel like I'm going to vomit.

He takes a deep breath and holds his hands up in surrender. I stand opposite him, terrified I may have started something that's way beyond my sixteen years.

"I'm sorry, I'm sorry. I hope I didn't hurt you." He looks at the hand I'm flexing to work the circulation back in to, the wrist a deep shade of crimson. "I'm sorry."

I cradle my throbbing hand to my chest. "Please, let me go. I want to go."

"You're so beautiful and innocent. I just wanted to spend some time with you before..."

"Before what?" My young mind is having a hard time computing what's going on. His eyes are manic, unfocused, and glassy. "Are you okay?"

He takes a few steps toward me, still holding his hands up. "I just want to make things right with you, is that okay? Can I come close?"

I'm suddenly frozen, doing nothing to stop him from coming closer. As he runs his hands up and down my arms in a show of comfort, my head screams at me to run, but my heart is relishing in the feel of his eighteen-year-old hands on me.

"You like when I touch you? Feeling my hands on you? My breath on your skin?"

Closing my eyes, lost in the heady fog his touch and words are creating, I don't even realize that we move until I'm pinned between him and the door. He trails kisses down the column of my neck while his hands skate up my legs, slipping under my skirt. I try to halt his movement, but he just shoves my hands away.

I open my eyes to see his pants are around his knees, his cock bobbing against his stomach. His lips are now pressed against my ear, whispering, "So damn beautiful," as he gives me most of his body weight while pushing my skirt up to my waist.

"No. Please, Thomas, not like this. Please, I'm not ready for this." I look him in the eye, hoping my desperation sparks something inside of him to stop this.

He pries my thighs apart forcefully and moves my

panties to the side before driving himself inside me. I try pushing him off, but it only seems to excite him more.

With one hand, he manages to pin my hands above my head, and the other he uses to cover my screams as he picks up speed.

Something foreign begins to stir, causing a warm sensation to take over my body. My heart kicks up to a rapid beat—not in fear...but *pleasure*? How could I possibly enjoy what he's taking from me against my will?

I begin to pulse around his cock, and this makes him smile.

"You're gonna love what comes next."

Maybe if I close my eyes, if I concentrate hard enough, I can stop the impossible.

"Oh yeah, come for me, Keely," he grunts as he pumps once, twice, and then silently releases inside me. The quiver I feel between my legs starts off as a tremble and sends me soaring over the edge in a tsunami size wave.

Wordlessly, he drops my legs, pulls out and tucks himself inside his jeans. I can't breathe, let alone move. I stand there, watching him step back from me like what just happened was an everyday occurrence. The stickiness between my legs is starting to trickle down my thighs.

"Don't look so horrified, Keely. You got off just like I did. Nothing bad happened if you enjoyed it." He points toward my legs. "You might want to clean yourself up before coming back up."

I wait until he opens the door I'm standing beside, walks though without a second glance and leaves before I look down to my thighs. His release slowly makes its way down my legs, mixed with blood, leaving a pink smear in its path.

It takes me over an hour to clean up and collect myself enough to walk out the patio doors where the party is now in full swing.

"Sweetheart, there you are. Where have you been? You missed the announcement." My mother throws her arm over my shoulder, tucking me into her side. "Honey, this is Larry. Larry, this beautiful girl is my Keely Jane."

Larry, standing a few inches shorter, and about fifty plus pounds heavier than my mother, extends his hand. "It's a pleasure to finally meet you, Keely. You and your sister are all your mother talks about."

I just stand there, not responding to the offer of a friendly handshake.

"Keely, you're being rude." Mom squeezes my shoulder to get my attention.

"Oh, honey, it's okay. It must be difficult meeting new people." Larry's smile grows as I feel a presence behind me. "I'd like you to meet my son, Thomas."

I look over my shoulder and see Thomas, beer in one hand, his other hand in his jeans pocket, looking completely relaxed. "You must be Keely. Nice to finally meet you."

"Now that the kids have met, I have a couple I want to introduce you to." Larry grabs the hand my mother has draped over my shoulder and leads her away.

Thomas comes to stand beside me as I look ahead. He takes a swig of his beer before bending down to whisper in my ear, "Bet you hate me now."

He chuckles, bouncing on the balls of his feet as he takes the few steps off the deck to the grass, fading into the bustling crowd.

I didn't know a young woman could grow a hate so raw and consuming in a blink of an eye.

I do now.

CHAPTER ONE

KEELY

"*H*e's gone, Keely. He's fucking gone and it's all my fault."

"Go pack your stuff, I'll get you on the first plane out of here."

"He just left. He saw us and he just left."

His constant mumbling wasn't helping the situation. I needed to light a fire under his ass, and fast. His despair was getting a bit much, so just like the kiss, I did the only thing that came to mind.

I slapped him, hard.

His eyes immediately came into focus. "Kee, what have I done?"

Helping him off the floor, I grab his elbow and wrist and pull him up. "Listen to me." I place both hands on either side of his face and pull him down to my level. "Go pack your shit. I'll call the airline to get you home."

He stares at me for a few beats, then turns and heads toward his room.

. . .

The image fades all too quickly when I suddenly become aware that someone is standing beside me. Lying on bed sheets that no longer smell of jasmine, but the floral scent of Bounce, I crack an eye open to see the blurry image of a set of knobby, pasty white knees.

Only one set of knees I know of that can rival those of an eighty-year-old man's... Nala's.

I lift myself off the bed, just enough to bring my arms up from underneath my stomach, and brace my weight on my elbows. I blink my eyes a few times to get them to focus.

"About time you woke up. I thought you were dead."

"Nala?" I tilt my head up to see my sister, dressed in a white wife beater shirt, blue boxer sleeping shorts, and her sandy blonde hair in braided pigtails that hang over her perky tits. "Where am I?"

"You don't remember?" She takes a sip of the coffee I'm desperate to grab from her.

"Where am I?" I roll on to my back and take in my surroundings.

The walls and ceiling are painted black. The bedside table and dresser on the opposite side of the room are fire engine red. The bedding I'm cocooned in is silver. When I look over the side of the bed, I see a black garbage container filled with what looks like vomit.

"Is that from me?"

Nala sits on the bed, bouncing a couple times, sending wave after wave of nausea through my tired and worn body. Not to mention, the blinding daylight that's bouncing off every lacquered surface and hitting the back of my retinas.

"Could you close the blinds, please?"

"Uh-uh. We need to talk, and you need to stay awake."

"At least give me some coffee."

Nala leans toward the bedside table, grabs a Starbucks size coffee mug and hands it to me. "How are you feeling?"

Blowing on the piping hot liquid, I follow the dancing streams of steam before turning my attention to my very unimpressed little sister. "Like I've been beat by a drunken midget."

"What?" Her eyebrows crease. "Whatever. So tell me, who's Rourke?"

I take a sip of coffee and wait for it to settle my stomach acid. "Rourke?"

"Do you not remember anything from yesterday?" She crooks her leg up on the bed, facing me head-on.

"Should I?"

"Well, you called me a few days ago saying you were getting on a plane to come home. When I met you at the airport, two stewardesses had to help you off the plane and into a waiting wheelchair. The entire cab ride here you talked about fucking up with Rourke and that you loved him."

She takes another sip of her coffee while she waits for me to answer.

At first, the image of me being led to my seat on the airplane flashes minutely, and then the constant flow of alcohol in those tiny little bottles flashes in quick succession until I recall the entire flight home like a real-time movie.

When I fuck up—and this was a massive fuck up on my part—I self-destruct. The evidence is now sitting in the garbage can by the bed.

"Oh God."

"Yeah. You've been out for a day and a half now. I'm not sure how much longer I can hold Mom back from busting down my front door."

A new wave of nausea hits, along with a massive hot flash. I am no longer human. I place the mug on the floor just in time to start dry heaving into the garbage can.

"Great to have you home, big sis. Wish I could stay and watch you die, but I got classes, and then I have to work tonight." She gets off the bed and walks to the door. "I left you a little present on the windowsill. Make sure to crack the window open before you spark up."

Once the dry heaving subsides, I hang my head over the side of the bed to see the door close behind her. Wiping my mouth with the back of my hand, my eyes focus on the window that's above the dresser. Not so much the window itself, but the ashtray with something white resting on top.

I love my sister.

Pulling the sheets back, I roll onto my side to kick my legs out of the sheets and get to a sitting position. Once my head stops spinning, I shuffle one foot in front of the other and sit on top the dresser, crack the window open and light up the joint.

The instant calm throughout my body is a welcome feel after the last few days I've had. I bring my knees up to my chest, tapping the balls of my feet on top the dresser while I take my time, savoring every mind-numbing hit.

I'm so glad to be home.

§

Down The Rabbit Hole by Joz Maxel is **AVAILABLE NOW!**